DO

BEGINNING TO END!

PLANT yourself right here!

You've just entered the E. Ville Creeper Botanical Gardens on a school field trip. And today's lesson is this: Plants can be deadly!

There's a killer plant virus going around. Touch an infected plant and your skin will turn to scaly bark, you'll put down roots, and morph into a plant! And, once you're a plant, watch out for insects — especially the giant insects that roam these gardens!

This creepy field trip is all about you. You decide what will happen — and how terrifying the scares will be.

Start on PAGE 1. Then follow the instructions at the bottom of each page. You make the choices. If you choose well, you'll survive — and maybe even save your classmates. But if you make the wrong choice . . . well, those plants will love the way you taste!

SO TAKE A DEEP BREATH. CROSS YOUR FINGERS. AND TURN TO PAGE 1 TO *GIVE YOURSELF GOOSEBUMPS!*

READER BEWARE —
YOU CHOOSE THE SCARE!

Look for more
GIVE YOURSELF GOOSEBUMPS adventures
from R.L. STINE:

#1 Escape from the Carnival of Horrors
#5 Night in Werewolf Woods
#10 Diary of a Mad Mummy
#15 Please Don't Feed the Vampire!
#20 Toy Terror: Batteries Included
#21 The Twisted Tale of Tiki Island
#22 Return to the Carnival of Horrors
#23 Zapped in Space
#24 Lost in Stinkeye Swamp
#25 Shop Till You Drop . . . Dead!
#26 Alone in Snakebite Canyon
#27 Checkout Time at the Dead-end Hotel
#28 Night of a Thousand Claws
#29 Invaders from the Big Screen

Special Edition #1 Into the Jaws of Doom
Special Edition #2 Return to Terror Tower
Special Edition #3 Trapped in the Circus of Fear

R.L. STINE

GIVE YOURSELF

Goosebumps®

YOU'RE PLANT FOOD!

AN
APPLE
PAPERBACK

SCHOLASTIC INC.
New York Toronto London Auckland Sydney

A PARACHUTE PRESS BOOK

No part of this publication may be reproduced in whole or in part, or stored in a retrieval system, or transmitted in any form or by any means, electronic, mechanical, photocopying, recording, or otherwise, without written permission of the publisher. For information regarding permission, write to Scholastic Inc., Attention: Permissions Department, 555 Broadway, New York, NY 10012.

ISBN 0-590-41974-9

Copyright © 1998 by Parachute Press, Inc. All rights reserved. Published by Scholastic Inc. GOOSEBUMPS is a registered trademark of Parachute Press, Inc. SCHOLASTIC, APPLE PAPERBACKS, and associated logos are trademarks and/or registered trademarks of Scholastic Inc.

12 11 10 9 8 7 6 5 4 3 2 1   8 9/9 0 1 2 3/0

Printed in the U.S.A.   40

First Scholastic printing, September 1998

"Whoa!" you exclaim as the school bus pulls up to the E. Ville Creeper Botanical Gardens. "What a creepy place!"

Behind a tall, wrought-iron gate looms the oldest-looking building you've ever seen. Damp green moss and thorny, twisting vines cling to the ancient walls. Shrubs and thick bushes line a crumbling cobblestone path.

"Yeah," your best friend, Kerry, agrees. "It looks abandoned or maybe even . . . haunted."

You stare at Kerry, eyes wide. "I can't wait!" you and Kerry shout at the same time. You slap high fives.

"This is going to be the best field trip!" Kerry adds.

Famous last words . . .

Turn to PAGE 2.

"Okay, we're here! Everybody off the bus!" your teacher, Mr. Denmead, shouts. Kerry brushes her strawberry-blond hair off her freckled face and grabs her backpack. You slip a small notebook and a pen into your jacket pocket.

"It's so cool that Mr. Denmead knows the people who run this place," you tell Kerry as you exit the bus. "I don't know anyone who has ever been inside. These gardens have been closed for as long as I can remember."

"I'm more excited about the prize Mr. Denmead is going to award the team with the best report," Kerry declares. "That team is going to be us!"

You roll your eyes. Kerry is a major brain. She's such a straight-A student you're surprised the teachers haven't made her principal.

Sometimes she can be a little too enthusiastic, in fact. After all, how thrilled can you get over homework?

You're more interested in exploring cool new places. "Well, I can't wait to see what kind of weird plants they have. The weirder the better!"

"Kids, gather around." Mr. Denmead stands by the huge, rusty gates. "I have to warn you about something."

Turn to PAGE 3.

"We are here by special permission, so I expect you all to be on your best behavior," Mr. Denmead declares.

You glance around at your classmates. Everyone nods. You snort. As if anyone would admit they were going to get into trouble, you think.

"There are some very unusual plants inside," Mr. Denmead continues. "Plants you've never seen before. You may be tempted to touch them. But don't!"

Mr. Denmead steps up to the gates. Metal screeches as he pushes them open. Your class follows him along a pathway overgrown with weeds. You reach the decaying front porch.

CREAK! The porch moans as Mr. Denmead steps onto it.

You glance down at his feet. Something seems wrong.

Hey. The doormat — it's sagging in the middle. And the wood around the edges of the large mat looks rotten. Black spots and bits of moss stain the planks.

It looks as if the floor might collapse!

CRRREEAK! Mr. Denmead lifts his foot to step onto the mat.

"Watch out!" you shout. "The floor! It's breaking!"

Quick, turn to PAGE 134.

You gape at the room in amazement. The tall, arched ceilings are covered in banners of mucus. Slippery slime icicles drip down from the ceiling.

"What happened to this place?" you wonder. "Is it normal for it to be covered in slime? There's goop everywhere!"

"I don't know," Kerry murmurs. "I think something weird is going on. Something really weird! Let's get out of here!"

You hear a strange scuttling sound. Someone is coming.

"Quick — hide!" you whisper. "I don't want to get caught!"

You duck behind a slime-covered chair. Kerry kneels behind an old display case.

The sound comes closer and closer. From a dark hallway step three shapes. You stifle a horrified gasp.

They're monsters! They walk upright on two of their six legs. They have swollen, armor-plated stomachs, huge, glittering eyes, and sharp pincers. One of them carries a big rope net.

"They look like giant bugs!" you murmur in horror.

"Mutants," Kerry gasps.

You see one of the bug-monsters stiffen. It heard you!

It turns toward your hiding place. And points right at you!

Turn to PAGE 131.

"Kerry, let's check out the tropical exhibit," you suggest as you study the directory. "I want to see what kind of exotic stuff they have."

"Me too," Kerry replies. "I wonder if they have the famous tatlocus flower."

You stare at your friend. "The what?" Then before she can answer, you shake your head. "Forget it."

You follow the arrows down a long, dark tunnel. "I guess Mr. Creeper wants to save on his electric bill," you murmur. "I can hardly see." You don't want to admit to Kerry that the shadowy building makes you a little nervous.

You come to an old wooden door. "This must be it," you comment. You push it open.

And step into another world . . .

Turn to PAGE 113.

"We're locked in!" Kerry shouts. She pounds on the door with her fist. "What is going on?"

"I don't know," you murmur anxiously. "Who would lock us in here? And why?" You try to peer through the glass panels on the door. You use your breath to melt a spot in the frost so that you can see.

Outside the door, you discover that jerk Chris Nelson. He's doubled over, laughing.

"Chris did this!" you tell Kerry furiously. "I hate that kid! Hey!" You beat on the door. "Let us out!"

Chris doesn't even glance up. He's rolling on the floor.

"Come on! It's freezing in here!" Kerry moans.

Frost is forming on your clothes. Your teeth start to chatter. You don't have much time before you freeze!

"We've got to break down the door!" Kerry says through blue lips. "I saw a metal crowbar over there. Let's use it!"

"Maybe we could just turn off the air-conditioning," you murmur. You glance up at the huge cooling system hanging from the ceiling. "There must be a switch somewhere."

You're losing feeling in your feet. Decide what to do!

To break down the door, turn to PAGE 112.

To turn off the air-conditioning, turn to PAGE 79.

"Kerry!" you cry. "How did you get away from the turtle?"

She grins at you. "Easy. I whopped him a few times on the nose. It made him so mad that he swam away."

"Well, what are we waiting for? Free swim is over." You begin to paddle to the edge of the pond.

"Wait," Kerry calls. "I found something really cool down there. An underwater cave. You can breathe in it and everything."

"Cool!" you exclaim. "Do you want to go explore?"

"I don't know," Kerry replies. "That turtle is still down there. And we have to work on the report for the contest."

Then she shrugs. "I'll do whatever you want."

Hmmm, you think. I really don't want to face that turtle again. Especially now that he's mad.

But it would be *so* cool to check out the cave.

So what will it be?

To check out the cave, turn to PAGE 37.

To keep exploring the gardens, climb out of the water on PAGE 19.

The skull jumps again. Its pointed horns pierce the air.

Kerry laughs behind you.

"What's so funny?" you demand. You keep an eye on the jumping skull.

"I'll show you." She bends down and picks up the skull.

"Be careful!" you warn.

But Kerry points at the ground where the skull had been. You see a tiny gray mouse. It scurries away.

"The mouse must have been trapped under the skull," Kerry explains. "The mouse made the skull jump when it was trying to get out. I'm sure the mouse was a lot more scared than you were." She gives you a smirk.

"Ha-ha," you grumble. Kerry tosses the skull to you. You notice a tiny cactus growing in one of the eye sockets. "Cool!" you exclaim. "Here's the plant I'm going to study."

You point at the little cactus. But by mistake you poke it.

"Ow!" you exclaim. "I pricked my finger."

Suddenly you feel dizzy. The room starts spinning. Bright lights flash in your head. You feel sick. You fall to your hands and knees, dropping the skull.

"What's happening to me?" you cry.

Turn to PAGE 55 to find out.

"There must be some way to check out the inside of this place," you whisper. "Even if it's just for a little while."

You notice an open window farther down. It would be easy to climb in. "We could go through that window," you suggest.

"Look," Kerry whispers, nodding toward the front door. "The front door is open a crack. We could jump over the hole and go right in."

"Yeah, but then everybody would see us," you point out. "That creep Chris Nelson would probably tell on us."

You both glance over at Chris. He's picking his nose. As usual. Gross!

"You're right, he would squeal," Kerry agrees. "But if anyone sees us going through the window, we could be in even bigger trouble."

"That's true," you answer. You chew on your fingernail. You're dying to get in there and explore!

"Listen, I'll do whatever you want," Kerry concedes. "But decide fast. Before Mr. Denmead gets back and calls the whole trip off!"

Quick! Choose! To climb in the window, turn to PAGE 43.

To open the front door, turn to PAGE 87.

"We tried to save them. . . ." you begin.

"But we got trapped by these vines. . . ." Kerry explains.

Mr. Denmead gazes down at you sternly. "You mean to tell me you left them there?" he demands.

"B-b-but w-w-we —" you sputter.

"No excuses! If you handed in an incomplete assignment I would fail you, wouldn't I?" He glares at you and then at Kerry. "Well, wouldn't I?"

"Yes," you mumble. Kerry nods.

"Kerry, I'm especially surprised at you," he states. "You of all people should know better."

Your friend flushes a deep red. She must be feeling really bad, you think. She's never been in trouble before.

"Now you march back out there and finish this project," Mr. Denmead orders.

You stare at him. You can't believe it! After everything you and Kerry went through! All the risks! The danger!

Kerry tugs at your arm. "Come on," she urges. "I never failed anything. We have to start over."

Well, you heard her. That's right. It's back to the beginning for you. And even though it bugs you, this isn't

THE END.

"Run this way!" Kerry shouts. She grabs your arm and drags you down a hallway.

The giant insects are right behind you! The scratching sound of their feet on the stone floor sends chills down your spine.

SNAP! You glance over your shoulder. The big bugs are snapping their pincers open and closed. *SNAP! CHOP! CHOP!*

"They mean business!" you yell to Kerry.

You and Kerry race to the far end of the hall. You see a passageway. Through the closest one you catch a glimpse of sand. It must be the desert exhibit! you realize.

Through the other doorway you see thick trees. The tropical exhibit! You could hide in the trees, but it's farther away. . . . Maybe you should bolt into the desert exhibit.

Which do you want to try?

The monsters are right on your trail. This is no time for indecision. Hurry! Choose!

To race into the desert exhibit, turn to PAGE 59.
To run into the tropical exhibit, turn to PAGE 75.

Your scalp prickles as the strange man moves toward you.

"Why, there's our host now," Mr. Denmead announces. He steps out of the circle of kids toward the mysterious figure.

"Hello there, Wally!" the strange man greets your teacher. "Welcome to the E. Ville Creeper Botanical Gardens."

"Kids, this is Max Creeper," Mr. Denmead declares. "The gardens are named after his dad."

"Hah!" You laugh. "Kerry, you were scared of nothing!"

You decide not to mention that you were a little scared too.

Kerry's face flushes red. "Well, he looked so weird over there in the dark."

Actually, he *still* looks pretty weird, you think. Max Creeper's long, tangled white hair trails down his back. Bits of leaves cling to it. Twigs and flowers poke out of the pockets of his filthy overalls. And you notice he's not wearing shoes.

What is with this guy?

Turn to PAGE 132 to hear more from Max Creeper.

You slam the door behind you. You and Kerry collapse against it, panting.

"Those turtles have a major attitude problem," you comment.

"Well, as long as they can't turn doorknobs, we should be okay," Kerry replies.

You shiver. "I feel totally gross," you complain. "My clothes are soaked and my sneakers are all soggy."

Kerry nods. "Me too. And everything in my backpack got all wet. I didn't expect to go swimming today."

You glance around. You're at the end of a long, dim corridor. "We better try to find our way back to the main hall," you declare. "Maybe we'll dry off a little on the way."

"I can just picture Mr. Denmead's face," Kerry moans. "He's going to have a fit when he sees us."

"He'll have a bigger fit if he can't find us when it's time to go home," you point out. "Move it."

Move it to PAGE 31.

14

You don't like the way Max is staring at you and Kerry. And you don't much care for the way the plants are creeping toward you.

"Uh, Kerry," you murmur. "We should get back to the group."

"I want to find out more about these plants," she argues.

She picks the worst times to be brave!

"And I will be happy to introduce them to you, my dear." Max Creeper drapes an arm around Kerry's shoulders. He brings her deeper into the huge room.

You follow close behind, shuddering as more and more plants surround you. You have the terrible feeling that Max doesn't ever intend to allow you and Kerry to leave.

"My friends are very anxious to meet their new companions," Max continues.

Kerry stops walking. She stares up at Max. "Their what?" she asks.

Finally! you think. Kerry's figuring it out. You only hope it isn't too late. "Kerry, run for that door," you shout, pointing at the far wall. "And don't ask questions!"

Race across the room to PAGE 118.

You frantically scan the room. You spot another door just a few feet away.

"Come on!" You grab Kerry's hand and race for the door. Plants chase after you, reaching for you with their leaves and branches. You manage to duck out of the way.

You fling open the door.

"No!" you hear Max shout behind you. "Not in there!"

You ignore him. You figure if he doesn't want you to go through the door, that's *exactly* where you should go.

You and Kerry dash into the room.

"Oh, no!" Kerry gasps. "More plants!"

She's right. The room is filled with plants.

But these plants aren't moving. They sit in pots just like normal plants.

But then you notice something scary. These aren't normal plants at all.

They're covered with red spots.

"The virus!" you gasp.

Turn to PAGE 116.

Your head whips around. You peer through the murky water, trying to see what made that splash.

Kerry! She jumped into the pond to save you!

She swims toward you. There's nothing you can do to help yourself. You're about to black out. You only hope Kerry can do something before your lungs burst.

You see her grab a stick floating nearby. She pumps her legs hard. In a few strokes she is beside you and the turtle.

WHACK! She slams the turtle on the snout with the stick.

Instantly, it releases you and snaps at the stick.

You kick your legs with all your strength. You burst through the surface and gulp in air.

"Yes!" you cheer. "Thanks, Kerry! I owe you."

No answer.

You gaze around. Uh-oh.

No Kerry.

Turn to PAGE 48.

You race down the hall. The walls pass in a blur.

You can hear the giant insects behind you. They emit shrill shrieks. They sound furious.

"I think you made them mad," Kerry huffs beside you.

You come to a fork in the passageway. There's a sign with an arrow pointing to the left that reads: TO THE ARCTIC EXHIBIT. Another sign pointing to the right reads: TO THE MOUNTAINS EXHIBIT.

A huge glob of steaming goop lands on the wall right in front of you. It eats through the wall!

"Gross!" Kerry screams. "What is that?"

"I th-think it's acid," you sputter. "They're spitting acid at us!"

Another glob of acid lands right next to your arm.

There's no time to think. You'll just have to go on luck.

Hurry! Find a coin and flip it! If it lands on heads, you'll go to the Arctic exhibit on PAGE 36.

If the coin lands on tails, race to the mountains exhibit on PAGE 66.

Claws, feathers, beak . . .

It *is* a bird! And it's attacking you!

It tears at your shirt with its claws and pecks you with its beak. Its little, *sharp* beak.

You shield your face with your arms. "Help!" you cry.

Kerry dashes over. "Shoo," she orders. She bats at the little bird. "Shoo!"

WHOOSH! Thousands of fluttering wings stir up the air. The room fills with colors as parrots and parakeets and toucans dart through the foliage. Straight toward you.

"Oh, no!" Kerry gasps. "Look at all the birds!"

"They're everywhere!" you yell over their screeching.

They scream at you. They fly by your head, staring into your eyes. Some hover, shrieking, right in front of your face.

That's weird. You duck out of the way of a toucan. They all seem to be screeching the same thing.

Could it be . . . a *word*?

"I think they're trying to say something!" you shout.

"Are you crazy?" Kerry yells back. "Let's get out of here!"

What are you going to do?

To stay with the birds, turn to PAGE 24.

To move on to another area, turn to PAGE 62.

"Let's not take any chances with that turtle," you decide. "He might have friends."

You and Kerry scramble out of the pond. You lie on the grass and catch your breath.

"Yuck," you complain. "I'm soaked. Let's hang out here until we dry off. I don't want to have to explain to Mr. Denmead how we got wet."

Kerry nods. "Me, either. I have a feeling that jumping in the pond is on the list of no-nos."

You and Kerry squeeze out as much water as you can from your clothes. You shake your head hard, spraying water from your hair. Finally, you feel dry enough to continue going through the rest of the gardens.

Turn to PAGE 100 and choose another area to explore.

"We have to find an antidote!" you yell.

"Maybe someone was in that room with the gray door," Kerry offers. "Maybe they can help."

"Good idea." You race down the hall. You throw open the gray door. It's a laboratory.

And there *is* someone in it. A tall scientist wearing a white lab coat and thick glasses looks up from her work. "May I help you?" she asks.

"My friend here is turning into a plant," Kerry cries breathlessly. "We have to find an antidote! Can you help us?"

"You mean this plant is actually a kid?" the scientist remarks in amazement. "This is thrilling! This is unbelievable! This is going to win me a Nobel prize!"

"I don't want to be studied," you tell the scientist. "I want to change back into a kid again!"

"What makes you think I care what *you* want!" the scientist says with a sneer. She grabs a remote control off a table and zaps toward the door.

You hear a click.

"We're trapped," you gasp.

Turn to PAGE 81.

You grab Kerry's backpack. "Take off your shoes," you order.

She stares at you — but she does what you say.

"Got it!" You hold up the thick clump of bouncy grass. You tear it in half. "Stuff it in your shoes," you tell Kerry as you kick off your sneakers. The two of you fill your shoes with the grass.

Max Creeper creeps closer and closer. "You'll be very happy here," he tells you soothingly. "Plenty of sunshine and water. Lots of fertilizer to make you grow."

"Sorry, Max," you declare. "We have other plants — I mean, plans."

You grab Kerry's hand and jump up and down. The bouncing grass is working! You bounce high, high, higher.

And then you bounce right over Max's head!

Turn to PAGE 130.

"Let's shout a warning," you whisper to Kerry. "Then we'll run away really fast."

"Well . . ." Kerry hesitates. "What if they . . ."

CREAK! You waited too long!

It's too late — Mr. Denmead has opened the front door!

The kids in your class catch one glimpse of the hideous bugs and scream with fear.

"Kids, get back!" Mr. Denmead yells. But the monsters throw the net over your class and pull hard. All the kids fall to the ground in a heap. Mr. Denmead is in there too.

You and Kerry duck back down in your hiding places.

"They got everybody!" Kerry moans.

"We didn't help at all!" you remark sadly.

"We didn't have a chance!" Kerry adds.

The giant insects drag the net over the ground. They are headed for a big stairway.

"Help!" the kids scream. "Somebody help us!"

"Okay," you whisper to Kerry. "We've got to save them. Let's follow and see where the giant bugs are taking them."

Turn to PAGE 69.

"Why do they have a native exhibit?" you complain. "I can study local plants in my own backyard!"

"We have to take notes for our report on something in there," Kerry replies. "Might as well be now."

"Okay," you grumble. "I know you want to win that stupid contest."

"It's not stupid," Kerry huffs.

You and Kerry find the door to the exhibit. You push it open and step into a beautiful outdoor garden. Fruit trees stand in two rows. A small field of red and pink tulips borders a large pond. Lily pads float serenely on the pond's smooth surface.

"Okay, maybe this is nicer than my backyard," you admit.

That's when you notice a spectacular rosebush. Fat, colorful roses seem to burst from the branches. Only you've never seen roses *these* colors before.

Some are orange, some brown, some bright blue. Hey! They look just like the roses in that GIVE YOURSELF GOOSEBUMPS book *Secret Agent Grandma*, you realize.

So does that mean you should step up to the rosebush? Or run away as fast as you can?

Well? Have you read the book?

To run away from the roses, turn to PAGE 123.
To take a closer look at the roses, turn to PAGE 85.

24

"Come on!" Kerry shouts. "We've got to go!"

"No!" you declare. "I know the birds have something to say. I just have to figure out a way to understand it."

You think and think. But you can't concentrate because the birds are so loud. They're driving you nuts!

"QUIET!" you shout in exasperation.

It works! The birds stop their squawking. It's totally silent in the tropical exhibit.

"Wow!" you exclaim. You're so surprised that the birds obeyed you, you're not sure what to say. "So, uh, were you guys trying to tell us something?"

Kerry laughs. "Duhhh! Birds don't talk!"

You feel the blood rushing to your face. It *is* kind of a dumb idea. . . .

Then a little yellow canary lands on Kerry's shoulder. And puts its beak up against her ear.

Turn to PAGE 117.

You open your eyes. Everything is dark.

"Kerry?" you call. "Are you here?"

"Yes! I'm here!" she calls back. "What happened?"

"The monsters knocked me out," you tell her. You sit up.

"That's what must have happened to me too," she says. "I was fighting one minute, and then the next thing I knew you were calling my name."

"We've got to figure out where we are and how to get out!" you exclaim. "Let's feel around for a light switch."

You get up onto your hands and knees and start to feel along the ground. You're trying to find a wall.

Your hand brushes something soft. It feels like a big pillow or something, except it's sort of . . . fleshy.

"I found the lights!" Kerry cries.

The lights flash on.

And you see what you're touching.

Check it out on PAGE 65.

I better tell Mr. Denmead about this virus, you decide. I'd feel terrible if something bad happened.

Your classmates are gathered around Mr. Denmead. You and Kerry push through the crowd.

"Mr. Denmead," you call, trying to get the teacher's attention. "Mr. Denmead. Hey —"

A sharp nudge in your side cuts you off.

"Why did you poke me?" you ask Kerry.

She nods toward a far corner of the huge hall.

You peer into the dim light. You can just make out the silhouette of a small man. He crouches in a shadowy corner — as if he didn't want anyone to see him.

"He's been watching all this time," Kerry whispers.

A chill passes over your skin. "You mean — spying on us?"

"I don't know," Kerry replies. Then she gasps. "Look! He's coming toward us!"

Hurry and turn to PAGE 12.

"I swear, we're not plant thieves!" you babble. "We thought it was okay to take little samples."

"Well, you thought wrong!" Creeper snaps. "You two *are* plant thieves! You're not students at all!"

He's crazy! you think. He's totally insane!

"We *are* students and we can prove it!" Kerry says. "Ask us anything you want! We spent all day studying this place."

"Okay." Mr. Creeper's eyes narrow craftily. "You said you went to every area. Well, I'll ask you five yes-or-no questions. They will prove if you're telling the truth. . . ."

Mark down your answers to Mr. Creeper's questions.

1. Did you see any Arctic moss?   YES ( ) NO ( )
2. Did you see any rosebushes?   YES ( ) NO ( )
3. Did you drink anything?   YES ( ) NO ( )
4. Did you meet any slugs?   YES ( ) NO ( )
5. Did you meet any birds?   YES ( ) NO ( )

If you answered yes to all five questions, go to PAGE 60.

If you answered yes to four or fewer, go to PAGE 57.

The cutters may not be strong enough to cut those thick fibers, you decide. You grab the weed spray.

"Hurry!" Kerry wails. "It's smacking its lips!"

"Plants don't have lips," you assure her. You glance up at the ceiling.

Oops. Looks like you're wrong. The plant is licking its pointy teeth with its slick black tongue.

You have no time to lose. You take aim and — fire!

A thick cloud of purple gas envelops the plant.

The plant contracts violently, jerking Kerry hard. Then it coughs and gasps. A few streamers relax their hold a bit.

Yes! The plant is weakening. You spray it again. And again. And again.

Hey — don't you think you're overdoing it? Sure, you kill the plant. But you and Kerry breathe in that junk too.

Talk about toxic! You and Kerry are overcome by fumes.

If you ever wake up you should study the dangers of herbicides. Because if you knew more about them, you wouldn't have inhaled megadoses of poison. And this wouldn't be

THE END.

You gaze out over the pond.

Then you notice something under the surface. Something small and round. A black circle.

With a swish, the circle blinks.

It's an eye!

"Whoa! There's something alive under there!" you shout. "Kerry! Come check this out!"

You lean closer, trying to see what's in there.

A giant head bursts out of the water. You gasp.

Then you realize — it's just a turtle! You check to be sure Kerry didn't see you. You wouldn't want her to think you were afraid of a turtle. Even if it *is* big. Really big.

Besides, you weren't actually scared. Just startled.

SNAP!

You jump back. Hey! The turtle tried to bite your face!

You stare at the huge creature. It must be some kind of gigantic snapping turtle — maybe a mutant!

Then the turtle's huge, jagged beak clamps down on your shirt sleeve. It pulls you into the pond!

Quick! Turn to PAGE 46.

The room becomes very still. The plants must have heard you.

Kerry clutches your arm. Your legs tremble. How can this be? you wonder. How can plants move around on their roots?

How can those small trees be playing chess?

A voice interrupts your terrified thoughts. Max Creeper stands in front of you, grinning. "Welcome. I'm so pleased you found your way here. I was hoping someone would."

"Wh-wh-what's going on here?" you stammer.

Max smiles broadly. "These are some of my father's greatest works. Intelligent plant forms. And I've continued in his footsteps with my own experiments. We've made such progress in genetics. A little DNA from here, a little RNA from there — and *voilà*!"

Kerry releases your arm. She steps further into the room, her eyes wide. "You mean you've been breeding hybrids for behavior?"

Leave it to Kerry, you think. She can make the most amazing, unbelievable thing sound like homework.

"I grew up among these creatures," Max explains. "I prefer their company to humans. But I'm afraid they're bored. After all, I *am* getting on in years. They need livelier friends. Like you."

Turn to PAGE 14.

You and Kerry wander along the dim passageway. The tunnel twists and turns so many times, you have no idea where you are. You leave squishy, wet footprints in the muddy dirt floor.

"I wonder if anyone has ever been down here," you comment. You haven't noticed any other footprints.

"I wonder if anyone has ever gotten out," Kerry mutters.

Ugh! You wish she hadn't said that. "Lighten up," you tell her. "This is a really cool adventure."

Kerry makes a face at you. "Yeah, right."

You keep walking. Then Kerry comes to a sudden stop.

"Uh-oh," she mutters.

The tunnel splits into two branches. Kerry turns to you. "Which way should we go?" she asks.

You peer down each branch. "There's a staircase to the left," you tell Kerry. "But I hear voices to the right."

She shrugs. "You decide."

Head for the staircase on PAGE 128.
Follow the sound of the voices on PAGE 51.

You gaze at the directory. The air in the main hall is moist and stuffy. It gives you an idea.

"Let's go to the desert exhibit," you tell Kerry. "It'll probably be nice and dry."

"Fine." Kerry grins. "Just don't *desert* me in there."

You groan at Kerry's bad joke. Then you follow the arrows to a narrow corridor that branches off the main hall. You take about ten steps down the hall and notice a gray door on the right. The door is unmarked.

"Do you think this is it?" you ask Kerry. "Or do you think the exhibit is farther down the hall?"

"I don't know." She frowns. "It seems weird that the door isn't labeled. Should we peek inside?"

What do you think?

To keep on going, turn to PAGE 95.

To take a peek behind the gray door, turn to PAGE 74.

"Kerry," you whisper. "Do you still have that morphing plant sample in your backpack?" Maybe we can get the plant to morph into some kind of weapon, you think.

Kerry stares at you. She seems paralyzed with fear. You grab her backpack and dump everything out of it.

You can hear rustling behind you. Creeper and his plants must be moving toward you.

There it is — the frozen, morphing plant leaf.

You grab it and warm it in your trembling hands. You feel it begin to thaw.

You open your hand. The sample has already doubled in size. You glance up at the vine-covered door. "Turn into an ax," you urge the plant. "Or a saw!"

The plant shudders and oozes, stretching itself, growing larger and larger.

Will it work? Will the plant turn into something to help you?

Find out on PAGE 115.

"Good idea!" you tell Kerry. "We'll trick them." Seeing the larvae slam into the wall has given you an idea.

"Hey! Throw me your sweater!" you tell Kerry. She tosses her red cardigan to you.

You wave the sweater like a bullfighter's cape. You back up until your back is against the wall.

"Over here, worms!" you yell.

A larva launches itself through the air at you.

"Olé!" you shout as you whisk away the sweater.

The larva splats against the wall in a shower of pink goop.

It worked! You're psyched, although your stomach turns at the gunk sprayed all over the room.

"Gross!" Kerry shouts. "Do it again!"

You quickly "bullfight" the other two baby bugs. Soon you and Kerry are standing alone in a puddle of pink muck.

Turn to PAGE 93 to try to get out of the room.

"Yaaaiiie!" you yelp. You stare down at the door handle.

Only it isn't a door handle. It's a *hand*!

Long silvery fingers clutch you in their grasp.

"Wh-wh-what —" you stammer.

"The door!" Kerry yelps behind you. "It's changing!"

You raise your eyes from the silver hand to the door. You tremble with fear as you watch the door melt around the hand. It slithers off the wall. Then it rearranges itself into a tree.

A tree with a hand sticking out of the middle of its trunk.

Kerry's eyes widen. "It's some kind of weird morphing plant!" she exclaims. "Dr. Creeper must have invented it."

"Whatever it is," you cry, "it's not letting go!"

Turn to PAGE 39.

You duck down the hallway to the left.

"I guess we're headed for the Arctic!" you call over your shoulder to Kerry.

You see one of the gruesome creatures right behind her. Its pincers snap in the air. Its four spindly legs are outstretched, trying to grab her. Acid spit hangs from its face.

You've got to escape!

You reach a door of frosted glass. You kick it open and race into the Arctic exhibit. The ground is slick with ice. Kerry slides into the room right behind you.

The walls of the big room are coated with frost. Different kinds of Arctic moss cover the ground. Tall, spiky plants stand in a cluster right in front of you.

Behind you, you hear the first bug trip. It crashes to the ground, falling onto its round back. The second insect tries to help it stand up.

"Quick! Let's hide!" you whisper. You dodge around the spiky plants. You reach up to separate the stalks of the plant to peek through at the insects.

"NOOO!" Kerry screams. "Watch out!"

Race to PAGE 92 before it's too late.

"We have to scope out that cave!" you exclaim. "Let's go!"

You and Kerry dive back underwater. You follow her into a dim cave. Your lungs feel as if they're burning. Then you burst through the surface of the water.

"Air!" you exclaim.

"Cool, huh?" Kerry calls. She's treading water beside you.

You gaze around. Glowing purple moss covers the damp walls. Mushroomlike plants poke out of crevices.

And then — *SNAP!* A leathery beak chomps at your leg.

"The turtle!" you shout. You scramble onto a narrow ledge of rock. "He's back!"

"And he brought friends," Kerry gasps. "Lots of them!"

Uh-oh! You scan the cave. How can you get out without going back into the water?

Then you notice the outline of a door in the cave wall.

You don't have a clue where it leads. But the turtles are starting to climb out of the water after you. Snapping their beaks.

Looks like you don't have much choice.

You and Kerry dart over and race through the door.

Turn to PAGE 13.

"Give me the antidote!" you cry.

Kerry reaches into her pocket and removes the little glass vial. The green liquid shines inside.

"I'm so glad we went into that lab!" she exclaims.

Kerry uncorks the vial and hands it to you.

As you look at the green antidote you realize something.

"Oh, no," you moan. "I don't know if I'm supposed to drink it or rub it on my skin."

Kerry's face grows pale. "This is terrible," she wails. "If it's supposed to go on your skin and you drink it, it could poison you. And if you put it on your skin instead of drinking it, you're going to waste it all!"

She stares at you, eyes wide with concern. "What are you going to do?"

To drink the antidote, turn to PAGE 108.
To rub it on your skin, turn to PAGE 114.

You gasp as the tree changes shape again. It melts into a huge, spiky-leafed plant. The long leaves thrash in the air.

And wrap themselves around your body.

You tug and pull against the plant, trying to escape. But every time you manage to kick or hit it, the flesh of the plant melts away. It's like trying to fight a shadow.

"Help me!" you shout to Kerry. "It won't let go!"

"I don't know what to do!" Kerry yells.

You desperately scan the room. You notice a water pipe on the wall next to you. It's painted red with the words WARNING! HOT! in black.

If you could break the pipe, maybe the hot water would melt the weird morphing plant. . . .

"I know!" Kerry declares. "I have a thermos of ice water. The ice might freeze the plant — or at least slow it down."

You've got two plans to choose from — hot or cold.

The morphing plant squeezes tighter. Think! Think fast!

To break the pipe and melt the plant, turn to PAGE 122.

To have Kerry freeze the plant with ice, turn to PAGE 97.

"I don't want to go out in the hall. We might get caught," you tell Kerry. "Let's use the matches."

"Okay," Kerry replies. She walks over and picks up the matches from the floor. "But we need a strong flame. What should we light?"

"There's a stick over there," Matt says, nodding with his head. "Hurry! Those monsters could be back any second."

You know he's right. You run over to the stick and grab it.

"There are only three matches," Kerry worries.

She lights the first match. Her hand is trembling.

You hold the stick over the flame. Your hand shakes too.

"Careful," you gasp. But your breath puts out the flame.

"Come on!" Matt yells. "This is life or death!"

Kerry strikes the second match. You hold the stick.

"There it goes!" you whisper excitedly. So excitedly that your breath puts out the match again.

"Oh, no!" Kerry wails. "Those bugs are probably on their way back right now!"

"I'm sorry, I'm sorry!" you moan. "I won't say a thing!"

Kerry lights the third match.

You hold the stick out and . . .

Turn to PAGE 71.

You study the directory. "I didn't even know plants grew in the Arctic," you comment. "Let's go there."

Kerry grins. "Sounds cool to me."

"Kerry." You grimace at her bad joke. Then you follow the arrows to a passageway at the far end of the main hall.

It becomes very chilly. You notice that the stone walls of the hallway are covered in frost.

"Check out the door!" Kerry exclaims. It's a silver metal door with glass panels, like a restaurant refrigerator.

You pull open the door. It comes undone with a loud sucking sound. You step inside. Icicles hang from the ceiling in long, sharp daggers. In the middle of the room is a large pond of ice.

"It's so cold!" you murmur. Your breath forms a cloud.

SLAM! The door crashes shut behind you.

CLICK! It sounds as if someone just locked you in!

"What's going on?" Kerry cries with alarm.

You rush to the door. It *is* locked . . . and you're trapped!

Panic rises in your chest. You pound on the door.

"We're going to freeze!" you exclaim.

Hurry to PAGE 6.

"How are we going to get out?" Kerry moans.

The one remaining insect blocks the doorway. You glance around. Beside a big red fire extinguisher you notice — a door! It's labeled EMPLOYEES ONLY.

"This way!" you shout. You race across the Arctic exhibit. You fumble with the doorknob. Your hands are so cold your fingers don't seem to be working.

The giant mutant screams behind you. *Right* behind you.

Pure terror nearly blinds you. Your body trembles as you realize you're cornered. Kerry quivers beside you.

You bang against the fire extinguisher. It gives you an idea. Maybe spraying the monster would give you time to escape!

You lift the heavy canister, pull out the nozzle, and fire. Foam splatters over the vicious, angry insect.

The bug lets out a terrifying screech. It crashes to the ground, flailing its arms. You're amazed.

"The foam is hurting it!" you gasp. A terrible hiss rises as the foam eats away at the mutant's body.

"It's dead!" Kerry exclaims. You're so psyched!

Then, from behind the EMPLOYEES ONLY door, you hear a muffled cry.

Turn to PAGE 99 to see who's behind the door.

"Let's go in the window," you decide. "We'll be careful."

"Okay," Kerry agrees. "Come on."

Together, you sneak over to the window. You make sure no one is watching. Then you climb inside.

You're standing in the main hall. Faint light shines through grime-streaked windows. In the dim glow you see thick vines climbing the marble walls. Moss sprouts from the tile floor.

"Wow!" you gasp. "This place is wild!"

"Cool!" Kerry exclaims. She wanders off to check out a tree.

"Hey, how did you get in ahead of us?" an annoying voice whines behind you.

You spin around. It's Chris. The rest of your class swarms into the huge main hall.

"You didn't come in the back door like we did!" he says suspiciously. "So how *did* you get in?"

"None of your business," you snap. Chris is one of those kids who always wants to tag along. And if you don't let him, he figures out some way to get you in trouble.

I better disappear before he asks if he can hang out with Kerry and me, you think. That's the last thing you want on a field trip. To be stuck with Chris!

Sneak away quickly to PAGE 107.

"You're right," you tell Kerry. "These bushes are so thick they'll never notice us sneak past. Come on!"

You creep through the shiny leaves and twisting vines. You're almost at the door when — *BONK!* Your head bangs into something hard and round.

You glance up. *GULP!* It's the belly of one of the monster insects.

It bends down to grab you. You push it as hard as you can.

The bug falls backwards. It lands on its back.

You watch amazed as the creature flails its arms.

"It can't flip back over," you cry. "It can't get up!"

"Run," Kerry cries. "While we can!"

You and Kerry race to the door as the giant bug lets out a shrill, piercing cry. The other two insects rush over to it.

"Well, that bought us a little time," you pant. "Now what?"

"Let's try this way." Kerry points back up the hallway. You see another corridor to try.

"We've got to find the exit!" you shout. "Hurry!"

Turn to PAGE 17 before the creatures get you.

"Kerry, help me!" you shout. You grab the end of the table and heave it over.

Vials and papers fly everywhere. The heavy table flips over with a crash.

Good news! One of the flying bottles hits the scientist on the head. She's out cold!

Bad news! When the table crashes to the ground, it lands on the remote. It's smashed!

There's no way to get the door open.

You're locked in with the scientist.

And when she wakes up, you'll discover what they mean by the phrase "mad scientist."

She's really mad . . . at you!

THE END

You tumble head over heels into the murky green pond.

Terror shoots through you. The water is so dark. You feel as if you're being dragged into a watery grave.

The snapping turtle's teeth grip your sleeve. Its strong legs plow through the water. You're dragged deeper and deeper into the pond.

Where is it taking me? you wonder frantically. How deep is this pond? You yank and pull, trying to break free. But the turtle's massive jaws are clenched tight.

I've got to get to the surface! you think desperately. I'm running out of air!

SPLASH! Something thrashes in the water beside you.

Oh, no. Could it be another giant turtle?

Turn to PAGE 16.

Kerry is right! The plant is absorbing the hot water through its skin. It expands, soaking up all the liquid like a giant sponge.

Then the plant begins soaking up objects too. The broken pipe. Kerry's backpack. The dirt on the ground . . .

Eventually, it soaks *you* up too.

So long, sucker! Or should it be . . . soaker!

THE END

48

"Kerry!" You tread water and peer into the murky depths. The turtle must have her, you realize with horror.

Now it's your turn to save *her*.

You take in a great big breath, squeeze your lips together, and duck back underwater.

But you don't see Kerry or the turtle anywhere!

You swim a few yards in each direction. The pond is much deeper than it looks. Your air begins to give out. You rise to the surface again.

You gasp and sputter. Panic makes it even harder to catch your breath. What has happened to Kerry? Is she down there somewhere — drowned? Is she turtle food? Is she —

"Aaaagh!" you shriek as water sprays everywhere.

"Aaaggh!" someone shrieks back at you.

Turn to PAGE 7.

You slam off the light and duck behind one of the pods.

Just in time. One of the bugs bursts in with another squirming kid in its hands. It flips on the light and loads the kid into an open pod.

You notice that there are two more empty pods waiting . . . one for you and one for Kerry. Yikes!

The mutant bug scurries out of the room and shuts the door.

You and Kerry crawl out of your hiding places. "We have to get these pods open!" Kerry declares.

"I have an idea," you announce. "Remember the garden clippers out in the hallway? Maybe we could cut the pods open!"

"I have a better idea!" Matt exclaims. "There are matches on the ground over there. Burn the pods open!"

If you use the clippers, you'd also have a weapon if the insects came back. But you have to go into the hall to get them. You might get caught.

Maybe Matt's idea is better. Fire would probably open the pods.

Probably.

To try the clippers, turn to PAGE 52.
To try the matches, turn to PAGE 40.

You stare at the directory in the main hall. "Hey, we did it!" you exclaim as you scan the list. "We visited all the exhibits! I can't believe we made it through them all."

"Yeah," Kerry agrees. "It was cool. But I think we have to tell Mr. Denmead not to bring a class here again. It was too dangerous!"

"Maybe." You shrug. "But you have to admit it was pretty cool too."

"We are definitely going to win that contest," Kerry gloats. "I wonder what the prize is going to be?"

"*I* wonder where everyone is," you comment.

Kerry peers out a grimy window. "I see Mr. Denmead and a bunch of kids at the front gate," she tells you. "We better go join them."

You and Kerry head for the enormous doors.

"Stop right there!" bellows a voice. A hand grabs your arm. Kerry's too.

"Ow!" you cry. "Let go!" Before you can see who it is, a bright light shines in your face. It blinds you!

"You're in trouble," the voice booms. "Big trouble!"

Turn to PAGE 124.

"Let's head for the voices," you decide. "Who knows where that staircase leads."

"Yeah," Kerry agrees. "And if it's like the rest of this place it's probably falling apart."

You and Kerry trudge along the dark passageway.

"My backpack is getting heavy," Kerry complains.

"Shhh!" You cut her off. "I'm trying to hear what they're saying."

The voices are getting louder. It sounds like someone is watching television right around the corner. You and Kerry hurry around the bend.

And freeze. Your mouth drops open at the amazing sight.

You stand at the edge of a large room. It's set up as some kind of recreation room. Ping-Pong tables, TVs, sunlamps, music. That's not what has you stunned, though.

The astonishing part is that *people* aren't enjoying the activities.

"Plants!" you gasp. The room is filled with plants!

Walking, dancing, *moving* plants!

Close your mouth before you start catching flies. Turn to PAGE 30.

"I think we should try the clippers," you tell everyone. "These leaves look easy to cut."

"There's no time to lose," Kerry says. "Let's go!"

"Hurry," some of the other kids urge you.

You open the door and step outside.

"Kerry, you keep watch," you whisper. She pokes her head out into the hall.

The creepy hallway is dark and dim — no bug monsters in sight. You see the clippers lying about fifty feet away. They're under a tangle of strange, bristly vine stalks.

You step cautiously out into the hallway. You run, being careful not to trip on any of the vines.

"Hurry!" Kerry whispers.

You grab the clippers.

They're stuck! The vine is holding on to them!

Then you feel something furry brush against your ankle.

"Whoa!" you gasp. It's the vine! It wriggles up your leg like a giant snake. It pulls you down. You land with a *THUMP*.

Then it drags you down the hall, away from Kerry.

"Help!" you yell.

Turn to PAGE 125.

You have to tell Kerry about the horrible *thing* that holds her trapped.

She's not going to like it.

"It's some kind of plant," you begin, staring at the gruesome thing that looks like a giant suction cup. "Uh, in the center are rows of, um, teeth. And it has a big, gross tongue."

Kerry's face grows pale. "What else?" she whispers.

"Uh, the green stuff hangs from the edges. I guess they're how the plant catches ... uh ... catches ..."

"Food!" Kerry finishes for you. "And that's what I'm going to be if you don't get me out of — aaaaggghh!"

The plant contracts, jerking Kerry a few feet up. Toward its deadly mouth!

"Help me!" she screams.

You glance around desperately. You notice a big can of weed spray sitting by the stairs. That might work.

But those giant weed cutters lying next to it might do the trick better.

Don't waste any time deciding. Pick something!

To use the weed spray, turn to PAGE 28.
To use the weed cutters, turn to PAGE 94.

All of the front porch wood is rotten. You fall right through!

You land in a heap on a cement floor. A bed of straw broke your fall, so you're not hurt.

That was dumb! you criticize yourself. Now what do I do?

It's dark, but you can tell you're in a basement. Old gardening tools lie scattered on the floor. Rusty cans of plant food are stacked in a shadowy corner.

You hear a sound from above you. You scramble out of the way as someone comes crashing down onto the straw next to you. Kerry!

"I leaned over to see if I could help you," Kerry says, rubbing her rear end. "And I fell in!"

"Are you okay?" you ask. She nods.

"I think we're in the basement," you add. You stand up and pace back and forth. You don't like cramped dark places very much.

"There must be a doorway or some stairs somewhere," Kerry reasons. "We've got to get back. Mr. Denmead is going to be mad."

You glance over to the far corner. "Over there!" you cry.

A staircase! Good!

Hurry over to the stairs on PAGE 98.

Your head spins. Bright colors flash and pop in front of your face. Your skin itches and burns.

What is going on? you wonder. But terror keeps the words stuck in your throat.

"Your skin!" Kerry gasps. "It's . . . it's *changing*."

You stare down at your hands. Your eyes widen in horror. Scales are forming on your skin. The scales get rougher until they look like bark.

Vines shoot out of your fingertips. Leaves sprout all over your arms and legs. You feel your hair growing.

You have no control over what's happening to you. It's like a nightmare! Your head feels as if it's about to split in two. Your skin itches so much you want to rip it off.

Then, without warning, everything stops.

Inside, you feel like your regular self. But you know that on the outside, you are far from normal.

Kerry's face is pale. Her eyes look like they're going to pop out of her head.

"Y-y-you're a plant!" she stammers.

Turn to PAGE 64 to figure out what to do.

"I'll press the W button," you decide. You extend your finger. It's blue with cold. You press the button hard.

A hum fills the air immediately. You feel a blast of hot air from the machine. It feels wonderful against your skin.

"It's working! The W must be for *warm!*" you say.

What a relief!

"It feels excellent!" Kerry stands under the vent, rubbing her hands as if the machine were a giant fireplace.

"Yeah," you agree. You climb off the boulder and bask in the heat from the vent. Your toes feel all prickly. "The heat feels great! Too bad we don't have any marshmallows!"

You scrape some moss off the rock. "Look! I even got my plant to study for the report," you say.

"Me too." Kerry holds up a small plant.

A big drop of water splashes onto your arm. Then another . . . then another. You glance up. You gasp.

The giant icicles hanging off the air conditioner are starting to melt.

And they're going to drop! Right on you! Your blood freezes in your heart.

"RUN!" you scream.

Race to PAGE 120.

"I got four yes answers," you tell Mr. Creeper.

"Me too," Kerry says. "The slug one is a trick, right?"

"You're right," Mr. Creeper admits. "I guess you aren't plant thieves after all."

Thank goodness! you think. I'm so glad we did a good job exploring this place!

"I apologize," Mr. Creeper says. "When I think about plant thieves I go crazy. Well, better go join your class."

You and Kerry hurry out of the gardens. And guess what! You write the winning report.

They announce the winning team at a special assembly. When they call your names, you and Kerry scramble onto the stage.

Mr. Denmead hands you your prizes: two cheap-looking medals. "And that's not all," he adds. "You two have won something very exciting."

You and Kerry glance at each other. You hold your breath, waiting to hear what you won. A free trip to an amusement park? Gift certificates from the mall?

Mr. Denmead beams at you. "You're both going to spend the summer as volunteers at the E. Ville Creeper Botanical Gardens!"

THE END

You snatch up the beaker of blue liquid.

"Take this!" you yell. You splatter the scientist with the blue goop. "Quick, Kerry, get the remote!"

Kerry darts forward. But the scientist is too fast for her. She grabs the remote from the table and pockets it.

The scientist throws her head back and roars with laughter. The blue stuff drips from her hair.

"This blue liquid is just a new recipe for herbal shampoo," the scientists informs you. "Nice try. And as for you," she sneers as she turns to face Kerry. "You'll be the control for all my experiments. That means that everything I do to plant-kid over there, I'll do to you too!"

Looks like you and Kerry are going to be staying in the lab for a long, long time. . . .

Might as well PLANT yourselves there!

THE END

"Head for the sand!" you shout. Kerry races into the desert exhibit. You skid into the room after her. You turn and slam the door shut.

"Help me!" you cry, throwing your weight against the door. The giant bugs bang the door from the other side. They push and thump against it.

They're too strong. You can't hold the door!

The door slams open and you fly backwards through the air.

Ow! You land right in the arms of a giant desert cactus.

I've got to get down! you think. Away from the monsters!

But you're stuck! Little prickly thorns grip your arms and legs. You can't escape.

Why are they just standing there? you wonder. Staring. What are they waiting for?

The hot sun of the desert exhibit beams down on you.

It's hot . . . so hot . . . too hot . . . you think.

Then the horrifying truth hits you.

Those insects have a perfectly good reason to wait.

Don't worry. They'll take you down before you get *too* hot.

They like their kid-kabobs medium-rare, not well-done.

THE END

"How many of those questions did you answer *yes* to?" Mr. Creeper demands. "And you'd better be right!"

"Five," you answer.

"Yup!" Kerry chimes in. "I said yes to all five too."

"Five? *Five!*" Mr. Creeper seethes. "That's wrong! You lied to me! There were no slugs! It was a trick question. Thieves!"

"No! I swear! We're not thieves!" you cry in horror.

You try to reason with Mr. Creeper, but he won't listen. He marches you both into a closet.

THUNK! He slams the door shut and locks it.

"What are we going to do now?" you moan in the darkness.

"Hey!" Kerry exclaims. "There's a door down here! It's some kind of a chute." You hear her open a creaky door.

"Let's go down it!" you shout. "Maybe we can escape!"

You and Kerry slide down the chute. *SPLAT!* You land in a stinky, steaming compost heap. You're surrounded by plant trimmings and garbage.

The worst part is, there's no way out.

Down there in the garbage heap, you miss your family a lot. Too bad you can't write them a *compost* card!

THE END

"The screams are coming from this way," you whisper to Kerry. You start down the dark, damp hallway.

You can make out shapes moving in the dim light ahead.

You tiptoe, sliding as close to the wall as possible. Silently, you draw closer and closer to the creatures. A pair of old garden shears nearly trips you, but you regain your balance.

Then you see one of the mutant bugs! Fear jolts through your body. The insect clutches Matt, one of the kids from your class. Matt is struggling to get free, but it's no good. You feel so bad for him. He looks completely terrified.

You watch the monster drag Matt through a door. After a few moments, the bug comes back out and goes down the hallway, away from you.

"Hurry!" Kerry urges. "Now is our chance to save them! While the bugs are gone!"

You sneak forward and peek into the room. It's pitch-black. You step inside. You can't see a thing. But you can hear the sound of people breathing.

"Hello?" you whisper.

Turn to PAGE 103.

The screaming birds fly all around you. Pecking. Clawing.

Kerry is right — you've got to get out of here!

"Come on!" you shout. "Let's go!"

Shielding your head with your arms, you try to run for the door. But with your hands over your face, you can't see. You're not sure if you're still moving in the right direction. You feel a rush of panic as you bump into trees and bushes.

"Which is the way out?" you cry.

"I don't know!" Kerry wails.

You trip over a branch and fall to the ground. You hear Kerry scream and tumble beside you.

Flocks of birds swoop down on you. They peck at your flesh. Their claws dig into your skin and tear your clothes. Feathers fly into your mouth and up your nose.

"Why are you doing this?" you scream at the birds.

Of course, they don't answer. Don't you know birds can't talk? And there's something else you should have figured out by now:

This field trip is for the birds!

THE END

"We'll never be able to get everyone out!" you declare. "Even with a wheelbarrow! We'll have to brush the slime off them."

"I hope it works," Kerry worries. "The effect of the slime seems really powerful. . . ."

She's right. None of your friends can move at all. They're paralyzed.

You get to work, scraping the slime off them with your fingers.

If only you had some gloves . . .

Because pretty soon you and Kerry find that your fingers are numb . . .

Then your whole arms . . .

Then your whole bodies . . .

You've always been a nice person. And trying to save all your friends was a really nice thing to do.

But you didn't do it in the smartest way!

So now you're a real, honest-to-goodness *numb-*skull!

THE END

"Are you okay?" Kerry asks you.

"No, I'm not okay!" you shout, gazing down at your leafy arms. "I'm a plant! This is awful! What am I going to do?"

"I don't know!" Kerry moans. "This place is so crazy! I wish we had never come here!"

"All right! Don't panic," you order Kerry. "We've got to turn me back into a kid!"

"Should we try to find Mr. Denmead?" Kerry asks. "Or should we try to solve the problem ourselves?"

Your heart pumps so hard you can hardly hear yourself think. But you'd better think — and fast!

To figure out what happened on your own, turn to PAGE 77.

To go get Mr. Denmead to help you, turn to PAGE 105.

It's a huge pink bug larva.

"Gross!" you shriek. You yank your hand away.

"Watch out!" Kerry yells.

The larva jumps. It turns its head toward you and — *CHOMP!* It takes a huge bite out of the air.

You leap back. You can't believe you were touching it! Eeeew! It's so revolting. You take a step back and stumble over another one. You scramble to your feet.

There are three of the disgusting creatures. One of them glides over the floor toward you. It moves like a snake. A fat, puffy snake. It lunges for you, baring sharp teeth.

"We've got to get out of here!" you yell. "These things are vicious!"

Kerry is trying to pull the door open. A larva slides at her and chomps the air.

"I know! I know!" she yells. "But the door is locked."

"There's got to be a way to fight them," you shout. You notice a length of rope in the corner. "Let's tie them up!"

"They might be hard to tie up. But I don't think they can see very well," she says as one of them crashes into the wall. "I bet we could trick them!"

To try tying them up, turn to PAGE 121.

To figure out a way to trick them, turn to PAGE 34.

You turn right, toward the mountains exhibit.

"This way!" you shout as another glob of the spit lands at your feet. You race toward the door.

The door is locked!

"Oh, no!" Kerry screams.

"It's a dead end!" you shout.

And you're right. Because there *is* no mountains exhibit in this place!

The insects close in on you and Kerry. Their pincers snap victoriously in the air.

This is truly a DEAD

END!

You don't want to let some little plant virus blow the field trip. Besides, you assure yourself, this poster has probably been hanging there for years. From when the gardens were still open to the public.

But, just to be safe, you decide to hide the poster from Mr. Denmead. You grasp it in your hand and pull.

It won't budge.

You try two hands. But the paper won't tear off from the nail holding it to the vine.

How frustrating! "Come out already!" you mutter. With a hard tug, you rip the poster from the vine. The nail clatters to the floor, leaving a big hole in the plant.

SQUIRT! A spurting red goo shoots from the hole in the vine. It hits your arm.

"Yeow!" you yelp. That stuff really stings!

And the plant keeps spraying the searing goo right at you.

Turn to PAGE 111.

You were right! The birds *are* trying to communicate!

You strain to understand their shrieks. It sounds as if they're all screaming "Pon! Pon!"

You address the birds again. "Are you trying to say 'pon'?"

The birds nod.

Amazing! You are actually communicating with birds.

Well, sort of.

You turn to Kerry. Her mouth hangs open in shock. "What do you think *pon* means?" you ask.

She shakes her head. "Pon . . . pon . . ." she mutters. Then she brightens. "Pond?"

"Something about a pond?" you ask the birds. "You want to warn us about a pond?"

But before you can get a response from the astonishing birds, Chris dashes into the exhibit area.

"Hey! Look at all the birds! Polly wanna cracker?" he shouts.

All the birds take flight and start screaming again.

"Let's go," you tell Kerry in disgust. "We'll never get any answers now."

Choose another habitat to explore on PAGE 100.

The huge insects gather up the net. Even though it must weigh a ton, they carry it easily.

You shudder. "They're really strong!" you observe.

The mutants carry the heap of kids to a huge door at the end of the hall. You follow the monsters down a set of stairs and into a dark hallway. The walls are cold and moist. Your classmates' cries for help echo off the walls.

You stay far behind them so they won't catch you. Just the thought of what would happen makes your blood curdle.

Kerry is right behind you. "How are we ever going to help them?" she whispers.

You hear a scuttling sound.

"Shhh! It's one of the bugs!" you quiet her. You notice a doorway to your right. It's marked NATIVE EXHIBIT.

"Quick! Let's duck in here!" you whisper.

You push open the door and slip past. Kerry follows.

You're in the middle of an outdoor garden courtyard.

But the weird thing is, there's a TV set up on the lawn. And it's playing a videotape!

Turn to PAGE 133.

Of course, you remember. The birds in the tropical exhibit. They were trying to say something about a pond. Could this be the pond they were talking — uh, squawking about?

"Kerry," you call. "Those birds were saying 'pond.' What do you think that means?"

Kerry glances up from her notebook. "I think it means you will find any excuse to avoid taking notes."

"No, really," you insist. "Maybe they were trying to warn us to stay away from this pond."

"Or maybe they were telling you to jump in it," Kerry snaps. "Like I'm about to."

"Ha-ha. Funny." You gaze at the lily-pad-covered pond.

Kerry is no help. You'll have to decide for yourself what the birds were trying to tell you.

If you think the birds were warning you to stay away from the pond, turn to PAGE 104.

If you think they were telling you to check it out, turn to PAGE 76.

The stick bursts into flame!

You take the stick and hold it up to the pod Matt is in.

You really hope this works!

POP! The pod bursts open. Matt tumbles to the ground.

Relief floods through you. "Excellent!" you exclaim. You run from pod to pod, holding the flaming stick up to the shells. Each pops right open. And the kids fall out onto the ground.

But the kids are not getting up!

"What's wrong with you guys?" Kerry asks. She tries to help Suzanne to her feet.

"I feel numb!" Suzanne moans. She flops to the ground.

"Yeah," Matt agrees. "I can't feel a thing!"

Kerry examines Suzanne. She runs a finger down Suzanne's arm. "Do you think it's this slime?" she asks. She glances around. "They're all covered in it."

You gaze at your friends. "All I know is, we've got to get out of here. Should we try to brush off the slime?"

"I don't know," Kerry replies. "Hey! There's a wheelbarrow over there! Maybe we should try to wheel them out."

To brush the slime off your friends, turn to PAGE 63.

To use the wheelbarrow, turn to PAGE 86.

Your body shudders. You can't control the violent shaking.

One of the leaves drops off. Then another. Then a vine. Soon all your leaves and vines drop away. The bark covering your body chips off.

"Yes! It worked!" You collapse onto the ground. Your muscles ache. You feel weak from the sudden transformation.

"Are you okay?" Kerry asks. Her voice shakes.

You nod. You feel too stunned to speak.

You can't believe it. Only seconds ago you were a plant!

After a few minutes, you feel less shaky. "Let's get out of here," you say.

"Do you want to tell Mr. Denmead what happened?" Kerry still looks worried. "Maybe you should go home. Or go to a doctor."

"Nah," you decide. "I feel fine now. In fact, now that I'm back to normal, it was kind of cool to be a plant."

"Whatever you say," Kerry murmurs. "So, you want to keep exploring the gardens? Should we go back to the directory?"

"Good idea," you answer.

Pick another area to explore on PAGE 100.

Mr. Denmead is leading the whole class into a terrible trap!

"We've got to help them!" you whisper to Kerry.

Her eyes are wide with terror. "But how?"

"I don't know," you admit. Fear makes your brain go blank.

"Well, they look like big beetles, right?" Kerry says. "Maybe we could flip them onto their backs. Maybe they wouldn't be able to get up!"

"That could work," you exclaim. You consider something else. "Or what if we sneak up behind them. Then when they open the doors we could shout a warning. Then we'll run back down the stairs and get out the way we got in."

"That's a good idea too," Kerry says. "What should we do?"

To topple the bugs over, turn to PAGE 106.

To warn your class and escape downstairs, turn to PAGE 22.

"I want to check out what's behind this door," you tell Kerry as you grip the handle. "Whatever it is."

You push the door open.

"Wow," you murmur. You've discovered some kind of lab! Steaming beakers stand in wire holders on a black table. Computer monitors blink on a desk in the corner. There's no one around.

Kerry dashes in. Figures. She loves labs.

You follow a few steps behind Kerry. The smell of chemicals hits your nose.

"Pee-yew!" you moan. "It stinks in here! Let's keep going."

"Not so fast!" Kerry whispers. "Look what I found!"

Check out what Kerry found on PAGE 110.

"Head for the trees!" you yell to Kerry.

SNAP! CHOP! The pincers behind you sound deadly.

As you race into the dense green foliage in the tropical exhibit, a chorus of birdcalls breaks out.

This was a good choice, you realize. There are so many trees to hide behind. You quickly duck behind a large palm tree. Kerry kneels beside you.

You watch as the three bug monsters start to search the bushes and trees. You're so scared your teeth are chattering.

"We've got to get out of here!" Kerry whispers.

"I know!" you murmur. You glance around, looking for ideas. The exhibit is basically a small jungle, with all kinds of exotic plants tangled together. You notice some vines hanging down from the trees.

"Let's swing on the vines!" you whisper. "We'll sail right over their heads and out the door!"

"The vines don't look that strong," Kerry answers. "Maybe we should just crawl past the bugs. The trees and bushes are so thick, I bet they wouldn't notice us!"

To swing on the vines, turn to PAGE 109.
To crawl past the bugs, turn to PAGE 44.

Those birds were probably suggesting we check out the pond, you decide. It has cool lily pads floating along its surface.

Maybe you'll find some frogs too. Of course, you're supposed to be studying plants, but they're *so* boring. All they do is sit there. You don't understand how Kerry can get so excited about a bunch of leaves.

You hurry down to the edge of the pond. You have to admit, it is pretty neat down here. Kind of quiet and mysterious . . .

Still, you'd rather be checking out something more lively than floating greenery.

Turn to PAGE 29.

"We have to figure this out!" you exclaim. "I don't want to waste time looking for help."

"Okay, let's think," Kerry mutters. She paces back and forth. "What could have made this happen?"

"I know!" you cry. "The cactus! I pricked my finger on the cactus!" You try to bend down to pick up the cow skull — but you can't bend anymore.

"Look!" Kerry gasps. "There are little red spots on the cactus. You must have caught the plant virus. It turned you into a plant!"

"We need an antidote!" you yell.

Hey! Did you pick up a virus antidote anywhere along the way?

If you did, turn to PAGE 38.
If you didn't, turn to PAGE 20.

The beast draws nearer. You and Kerry hold your breath.

It passes right in front of you. If you held your hand out you could touch it. But you don't. You don't move an inch. You're too scared to move!

As soon as the big bug is gone, you peer out into the passageway. Your pulse is racing.

It races double-time when you hear a scream. "Help!" someone cries.

You recognize the voice. It's Suzanne.

The giant insects must have captured your class. Your friends are in trouble!

"We've got to help them!" you exclaim.

Race to the rescue on PAGE 61.

"Let's turn off the air-conditioning!" you shout. "Otherwise we're going to freeze!"

The cooling system is up on the ceiling. You need something to stand on. You notice a small, moss-covered boulder lying off to the side of the ice pond.

"Help me move that rock," you instruct Kerry. You roll the rock along the ice until it's under the cooler.

You climb up and see a small control box next to a giant icicle. There are two buttons: One is marked with a W, the other has no mark at all.

"I don't know which button to press!" you moan.

"Well, just pick one," Kerry snaps. "We have no time to lose. Hurry!"

What could W stand for? you wonder. Water? Waiter? Whisper? Whistle? Wink? What?

If you can wink one eye or whistle, press the W button on PAGE 56.

If you can't wink or whistle, press the un-marked button on PAGE 119.

"Give me the rope!" Kerry commands. You hand her the vine rope. She tosses it into the air.

It sails over the pipe and lands back at your feet.

"Nice shot!" you congratulate her.

"Get going before these vines beat us senseless!" she shouts.

The vines whip furiously at you as you climb. But you reach the skylight. You pull yourself through. You are stunned to see that, instead of coming out on the roof, you wind up in a hallway.

You turn and offer Kerry your hand. You pull her out.

"We made it!" Kerry gasps.

"Yeah, but we're still in the botanical gardens," you declare. "The skylight was fake."

"Well, we have to go back and rescue our friends," Kerry says. "They're still trapped in those pods."

You and Kerry find a staircase. You head down to the level where you think you left your friends.

A shadow appears on the wall in front of you.

Your skin prickles as you recognize the shape of two sharp pincers. It's the shadow of one of the bug creatures . . . which is standing right behind you. And there are two more behind it.

"Kerry!" you shout. "RUN!"

Race to PAGE 11. Fast!

"What a lucky accident!" The scientist smiles broadly. "Now, come here, little plant-child! We've got lots of experiments to do!"

"No way!" you shout, horrified. You and Kerry back away from her. This woman is insane!

You glance at Kerry. Her face is white with fear. Her eyes dart around the room. She must be searching for a way out.

But the only way out is with the remote!

Somehow we have to get that remote to unlock the door, you think. You can tell by the expression on Kerry's face that she's figured out the same thing.

You glance around the room. A bubbling vat of blue liquid is percolating on a counter. You could throw it at the scientist.

Or you could push the table over on her and block her way!

Kerry moves close to your side. You know she'll back you up, whatever you decide to do. . . .

"Come here!" the scientist yells. "I'm not playing around!"

Then she lunges at you.

Do something! Fast!

To throw the blue liquid at her, turn to PAGE 58.

To push over the table, turn to PAGE 45.

You watch as the crack in the ice beneath you branches out in a million directions. You're horrified — but there's nothing you can do.

SPLASH! You drop into the icy water.

Aaaahh! It's so cold! You force your eyes open and peer underwater.

You spot Kerry pushing her way into a vent in the side of the pond. You swim over to her. You both wriggle along inside the vent until you come to a spot where you can breathe.

"It's f-f-f-freezing in here!" Kerry's teeth chatter as she tries to speak.

You nod, your whole body trembling with cold. You spot a grate overhead. "M-m-maybe we can c-climb out through there," you suggest.

"I'll do anything," Kerry moans.

With shivering fingers, you and Kerry manage to pry off the grate. You scramble up and out into a dark hallway.

"Wh-wh-where are we?" Kerry wonders.

You wonder the same thing. But you know you have to keep moving. You've got to warm up!

Turn to PAGE 31.

You gaze at the bookshelves. They reach practically to the ceiling. You'll have to stretch really far to reach the skylight. But you're sure you can do it.

And the shelves look a lot safer than those wriggling vines!

You and Kerry scramble up the bookshelves. You knock books to the floor, trying to get a handhold.

"Ugh!" You grunt and pull yourself up another few feet. Soon your hands start to hurt. Climbing is hard work!

Sweat breaks out along your forehead. It starts dripping into your eyes. Ow! That stings.

Something wipes the sweat off your face. "Thanks," you murmur.

Then you gasp. You just thanked a *vine.*

You're so shocked, you let go.

Oops!

And you were making such good progress. You were almost to the top.

Which means you fall a long, long, *loooong* way down. Which means this is

THE END.

You turn the combination to 0-0-8-4.

The door lock clicks. It worked!

"You owe me a million bucks," you joke to Kerry.

But as you grab the handle, *someone turns it from the other side*. You gasp.

The door opens. You gasp again.

It's one of the giant bugs!

"Help me!" you shout to Kerry. "Close the door!" You throw your body against the door, trying to shut the monster out.

But it's no good. The mutant bug pushes the door open and comes into the room. When it sees what you did, the creature lets out a long, piercing wail.

Mamas don't like it when you mess with their babies.

And monsters don't like it when you mess with their larvae.

Know what? You're in trouble. You're in a *larva* trouble.

THE END

"Those roses are incredible!" Kerry exclaims.

"Yeah," you agree. "And such weird colors!"

You step up to the rosebush. Some of the flowers are striped, some have polka dots. And they have an unusual odor — sort of like bananas! You step closer and take a whiff of an orange and green polka-dot rose.

That's when you notice the tiny eyes peering back at you from the blossoms.

"Aaaaaggghh!" You shriek and stumble backwards.

Admit it. You never read *Secret Agent Grandma*, did you?

If you had, you would know that some of these roses can behave pretty badly.

Especially when they're hungry.

And since no one has been to visit these gardens in a very long time, these roses are starving.

But not for much longer . . .

Yup, the flowers' future looks rosy. Filled with delicious meals. But things look pretty thorny for you and Kerry. . . .

CHOMP! Munch, munch, munch.

Talk about flower power.

THE END

"We don't have enough time to brush off the slime," you say as you hurry over to the wheelbarrow. "Besides, who knows if it would even work?"

You pull your friend Matt gently into the wheelbarrow. Then you wheel it over to another kid. You load her in.

It's hard work! Sweat pours down your neck and your back. Your arms shake. This is going to take a really long time, you worry. What if the mutant bugs come back?

You wheel the two kids toward the door. Kerry opens the door for you. She pokes her head out into the hall.

"The coast is clear!" she whispers. "I'll get ready for the next load. Hurry!" She drags another kid over to the door.

You push the wheelbarrow out into the hall.

"Be careful!" Matt whispers.

This is a bad idea, you realize with terror. The wheelbarrow is too heavy. You can't control it. It sways to the right, to the left, and crashes into the wall.

Right into a little red alarm box!

Your friends tumble to the ground. You watch as the box lights up. The alarm is going to go off and the bugs will get us, you think. We're all goners — and it's all my fault!

Turn to PAGE 89.

"Let's go in through the front door," you tell Kerry. "After all, it's open."

"Yeah," Kerry agrees. She turns to face your classmates. "Hey, you guys, we're going to go in and check the place out."

"Does anyone want to go with us?" you ask.

"No way!" Chris scoffs. "Are you two crazy? You're gonna get busted. So busted!"

"Whatever," you retort. "Come on, Kerry."

You stare at the porch, scoping out the distance you need to jump to clear the gaping hole.

"I think I should be able to make it if I take a step waaaay to the left, and then waaaaay to the right again," you tell Kerry. "That should put me right at the doorway."

She nods. "That will work. If your legs are long enough."

You stretch out your left leg. You clear the hole on the left side. You stand on one foot for a moment. You wobble and teeter. You fling out your arms wildly, trying to maintain your balance.

Phew! You plant your foot in front of the door. Made it!

CREEEEAAAAKKK!!!!

Uh-oh . . .

Quick! Turn to PAGE 54.

"Are you okay?" Kerry calls as she runs down the hallway.

You watch in helpless horror. You want to warn her — but the vines cover your mouth.

The vines grab Kerry. She's dragged into the library too.

The vines release you both. But they have blocked the door.

"Wh-wh-what's going on?" Kerry sputters.

"I don't know," you admit.

You and Kerry peer around the library. Bookshelves line the walls. But there are no other doors.

You notice a skylight far above you. You point it out to Kerry. It seems to be the only way out.

"Maybe we should try to climb the bookshelves to get up there," Kerry suggests.

You glance up to the ceiling and notice a water pipe near the skylight. It gives you an idea.

"What if we tied two or three of the vines together and made a rope!" you think aloud. "Then we could throw the rope over that pipe and climb out!"

"I'll try whatever you want," Kerry offers.

To climb up the bookshelves, turn to PAGE 83.
To make a rope from the vines, turn to PAGE 96.

The alarm box flashes.

And it starts to rain in the hallway and in the pod room!

You can't believe your eyes. You didn't set off a security alarm! You set off a fire alarm and now the sprinklers are on.

"Hey! I can move!" Matt cries. Shakily, he rises to his feet. "The water rinsed off the slime!"

You feel so relieved! What a lucky accident!

All the kids from your class swarm out into the hall. They're dripping wet from the sprinklers. They start to thank you for setting them free.

"Shhhh!" Kerry interrupts. "Quiet! We could be captured by the insects any second. We've got to get out of here!"

"Follow me!" Matt commands. "I remember the way out."

All twenty-eight of you sneak down the corridor. You and Kerry keep watch at the back of the group.

Matt leads the group into the main hall. You see the front door! Freedom is in sight!

"There it is!" you turn and whisper to Kerry.

But you see something behind her. Two clawed pincers!

A bug! Sneaking up! "Watch out!" you shout.

Race to PAGE 101.

"Yes!" you answer proudly. "We saved them! The giant bugs caught us when we were escaping."

"You two are really great!" Mr. Denmead beams at you. "You saved your whole class and you saved me too!"

You feel fantastic. You did everything right.

"We're a good team," you tell Kerry. You high-five.

You and Kerry are heroes. Everywhere you go people want to hear the story.

Over and over and over again.

In fact, you're kind of getting sick of it. How many times can you describe the battle of the bugs?

So you and Kerry decide to become famous for something else. But what? you wonder.

Guess you'll just have to have as many weird adventures as you can. Don't look at this terrifying episode as

THE END.

It's just the beginning!

"I'll try ninety-one," you tell Kerry. You turn the numbers to 0-0-9-1. Then you cross your fingers for luck and turn the handle.

It opens!

"I got it!" you exclaim.

"Wow! I can't believe it!" Kerry gasps. "You really are lucky."

You open the door and poke your head out into the hallway. The corridor is lined with dark, mossy stones. The air smells moist.

"We've got to find the main hall," you declare.

You notice a shadow moving against one of the walls. A *big* shadow, with lots of arms and two huge pincers.

"It's one of them!" Kerry hisses with fear.

A chill runs up your spine.

"Quick! In here," you whisper. You pull Kerry into a shallow doorway. You hope the creature won't see you there, pressed up against the damp stones.

You hold your breath as the monster scuttles closer.

Turn to PAGE 78.

"That plant is deadly!" Kerry races around the plant and stops you from touching it.

You take a good look at the plant. Tiny, pointed darts are hidden in the middle of the spiky leaves.

"This is a Juno dart plant!" Kerry whispers. "It can shoot darts up to fifty feet! Don't touch it!"

The insects struggle to their feet. So far they haven't seen you behind the deadly Juno dart plant.

The plant gives you an idea.

"Hey, bug-brain!" you yell, waving your arms. "We're over here! Come and get us!"

"Are you crazy?" Kerry hisses.

The two mutants hear you and squeal with anger. They rush at the dart plant.

"Duck!" you yell, pushing Kerry to the ground.

BAM! POP! POW! The darts fly from the plant. They shoot into the two insects. The bugs scream and fall to the ground.

"It worked!" you proclaim as the darts stop shooting. "Now let's get out of here."

•

Turn to PAGE 42.

"I am totally grossed out," Kerry mumbles, gazing at the muck on the floor. "Can we figure out a way to get out of here, please?"

"Just a second," you say. You bend down to examine the strange lock on the door.

"There's a combination lock on this door," you say. "It's got four rotating numbers — but it shouldn't take us long to figure out which numbers open the door."

"Are you kidding? It could take hours!" Kerry exclaims. "There are hundreds of possible combinations!"

You know she's probably right, but you feel confident you'll get the combination right away.

"Maybe," you tell her, "but ninety-one and eighty-four are my lucky numbers. I'll bet you a million dollars it's one of them!"

"Okay, go for it!" she tells you. "Try one or the other. But please hurry! I want to get out of here before those monsters come to check on us . . . or on their babies."

To try 0-0-9-1, turn to PAGE 91.
To try 0-0-8-4, turn to PAGE 84.

Those weed cutters should work! You grab the heavy shears and lug them over to Kerry.

"Hurry!" she cries. The plant contracts again. She's yanked up a few more feet.

"Don't worry, I'll cut you down!" You dash up the stairs. You strain to reach the strands that hold Kerry.

"Be careful," Kerry warns. "Cut the weeds — not me!"

You hold the weed cutter steady. You hope it's sturdy enough to cut through the thick fibers.

SLOP! THWAP!

"Hey! Ewwww!" you shout.

The disgusting tongue zips out and curls around the weed cutter. It yanks the tool right out of your hands. It tosses it down the stairs.

WHAP!

Then it goes for you! The slimy tongue wraps around you. It lifts you up to the hideous mouth.

CRUNCH!

Hate to tell you, but . . .

You're plant food!

THE END

"That looks like an office or something," Kerry declares. "Let's not bother with it."

You glance at the door again. She's probably right. "Okay," you agree. "An office would be boring."

You and Kerry continue down the hall and discover a door marked DESERT EXHIBIT.

"This is the place," you say over your shoulder as you push the door open. You're looking back at Kerry when she screams, "Watch out!"

Whoops! The warning came too late. You trip and go sprawling on the sand. You land hard.

And come face-to-face with a grinning cow skull.

"Ewww!" You scramble to your feet.

The skull twitches. And jumps into the air!

"Get back!" you cry.

Turn to PAGE 8.

"We'll never be able to climb the bookshelves," you tell Kerry. "Come on! Let's make a rope!"

You grab one of the vines. It twists and struggles in your hands. You snap it in two. It goes limp.

But the other vines start to move faster.

"I think you made them mad!" Kerry shouts.

You tremble with fear as the vines start to thrash in the air. They whip you! It hurts!

"Ow!" you yell. "They're going crazy!"

Kerry grabs a vine and breaks it in two. The other vines are furious. They flail and fly through the air. They beat you on the back. Kerry hands you the vine.

Breathlessly, you manage to tie the two vines together.

You and Kerry struggle through the tangle of furious vines until you're right under the water pipe. You throw your vine rope up into the air. It misses the pipe.

"Hurry!" Kerry shouts. "We've got to get out of here before the vines whip us to death!"

You feel panicked. The vines hiss and boil around you. They whip your arms and legs. You throw again. It misses.

"I don't think this is going to work!" you shout.

Turn to PAGE 80.

You remember something from science class. You hear Mr. Denmead's voice: *When a liquid cools, the particles slow down.*

The way the weird morphing plant moves makes you think it must be some kind of liquid.

So ice would cool the liquid and slow the plant down!

"Use the ice!" you shout to Kerry. "And use it quick!"

As Kerry digs the thermos out of her backpack, you wrestle the plant to the ground. It moves like Jell-O under you. Every time you think you have a leaf or a branch pinned down, it morphs!

"I can't believe this is happening!" you shout.

"Keep fighting it!" Kerry screams.

As you struggle, one of the branches takes the shape of a huge hammer. It rises into the air over your head. . . .

"Kerry!" you cry. "Help meeeeee!"

Quick! Turn to PAGE 126.

You both rush over to the old wooden staircase. The planks look split and rotten. Up at the top of the staircase you see a door. It's open a crack.

"These stairs are in worse shape than the porch," you say. "But I guess this is our only choice. I'll go first." You step up onto the creaking planks.

With every footstep, the staircase moans and trembles. But you reach the top safely. Whew! You wipe the sweat off your forehead with the back of your sleeve.

You push open the door. You step out into the main hall of the botanical gardens. The room is enormous. An incredibly fancy-looking entrance hall . . . except for one thing.

Your jaw drops as you gasp at the sight before you.

"Wow!" Kerry exclaims from behind you as she enters the room.

"Slime!" you murmur.

The huge room is totally covered in green slime!

Turn to PAGE 4.

You throw open the EMPLOYEES ONLY door. Behind it is a small room filled with filing cabinets.

Mr. Denmead stands beside an open file drawer!

"Mr. Denmead," you cry. "What are you doing in here?"

"Hiding from the insects," Mr. Denmead explains. "They didn't have a pod the right size for me, so they left me alone for a moment. I escaped and discovered these files. I was hoping they might tell me something about the gruesome beasts."

You glance back at the dead bug on the floor behind you. You shudder.

"I think we should leave before any more of those mutants show up," Mr. Denmead says.

"We got three of them," you boast.

"Congratulations! But before we go, I have to ask you a question." Mr. Denmead's face is deadly serious. "Did you two save the rest of your classmates or are they still in danger?"

Did you free your classmates from the pods or not? Tell the truth.

If you saved your classmates from the pods, turn to PAGE 90.

If you did not save the other kids, turn to PAGE 10.

THE E. VILLE CREEPER
BOTANICAL GARDENS

Please explore all of our exciting areas:

TROPICAL (Turn to PAGE 5.)
ARCTIC (Turn to PAGE 41.)
NATIVE (Turn to PAGE 23.)
DESERT (Turn to PAGE 32.)

Enjoy your visit and please
DO NOT TOUCH THE EXHIBITS.

Choose which region you want to explore. To write the best report and win the special prize, you'll need to visit every area. You can go in whatever order you like. But the order could matter, so think about your choices.

When you have visited all the areas, turn to page 50.

You race for the front doors. Matt gets there first and throws them open. All the kids from your class stream out. You tear toward the entrance-way. . . .

You're almost out! You're almost safe!

Two giant pincers clamp down on your arms and throw you backwards. You land on the floor with a sick *THUMP.*

"Noooo!" you hear someone yell.

A kid comes skidding along the floor and lands right next to you. Another captive of the insects.

You glimpse a familiar flash of strawberry-blond hair and freckles. It's Kerry! She peers up at you.

"This doesn't seem right!" she complains. "We save all the others and get trapped again? No fair."

The two giant bugs who caught you and Kerry start to scurry over to you. You scramble to your feet.

"Never mind fair!" you shout. "Run!"

Turn to PAGE 11.

You poke your head around the door of the native exhibit. "All clear," you whisper. You and Kerry sneak out.

"Now that we know what the creatures are," Kerry says, "maybe we can figure out a way to defeat them."

You gaze up and down the hall. "Which way do you think they went?" you ask.

Before Kerry can answer, you hear a scream.

"Help!" a voice shouts. "Somebody help us!"

"That's them! Let's follow the sound!" you exclaim.

Go find your class on PAGE 61.

"Who's that?" several voices cry out.

"It's me and Kerry," you announce. "Hold on!"

You reach out and brush the wall with your hand. You've got to find a light switch.

CLICK! You flick it on.

"Oh, no!" Kerry gasps.

The kids from your class have been loaded into weird plant pods. The pods are two leaves clamped together like clamshells. Your friends' bodies are trapped inside the pods. Only their heads stick out from the top.

A shudder crawls down your spine. This is major trouble!

"You've got to get us out of here!" your friend Suzanne shouts.

Then you hear the awful scuttling sound. Your stomach lurches.

One of the giant insects is coming back!

"Hide!" Kerry shouts. "Quick!"

Hide on PAGE 49.

104

You're not taking any chances. You decide to avoid the pond. Just in case the birds didn't want you anywhere near it.

So now what? you think. You scan the garden. You have to write about *something* in this stupid exhibit.

You cross the lawn, glancing around. You see lots of nice flowers, but so what? To win the contest you need to write something more interesting than *gee, pretty.*

You pace back and forth. The bright green grass beneath your feet feels springy. In fact, you realize, each step you take lifts you off the ground a little more.

Am I imagining things? you wonder. You peer down at the ground. Is this some kind of special bouncy grass?

You decide to test it. You jump up and down.

"Whoa!" you exclaim.

Each jump takes you two, three, even four feet into the air!

Bounce over to PAGE 135.

"We have to get help," you decide. "This is too serious to handle by ourselves."

"Okay. Follow me!" Kerry declares.

You try to follow her, but your feet won't move.

You stare down and discover, with horror, that your feet have become roots, digging far down into the sandy soil.

Oh, no! You feel yourself going into hysterics.

You pull. Frantic. No. They won't budge.

"I can't move!" you shout, terrified. "Kerry, run! Bring help!"

While she's getting help, turn to PAGE 129.

"Let's flip them over," you tell Kerry. "I don't want to try to outrun those beetles — they can probably move really fast."

"Let's get them!" Kerry agrees.

You race forward. You jump on the back of the biggest creature. It lets out a squeal of surprise. You pull backwards, trying to get it to topple over.

But it's got two of its six feet planted firmly on the ground. It grabs your arms with its pincers and swings you over its head. You dangle in the air in front of it.

"Let go of me!" you shout. You swing both fists. But they don't come anywhere near the big bug's face.

"What's going on in there?" Mr. Denmead shouts. You thrash your arms and legs. You're desperate to get away!

Then a hole opens right between the giant bug's huge, glassy eyes. A small feeler darts out at you.

ZAP! It shoots something into your neck.

"Nooo!" you shout. Everything goes black.

Turn to PAGE 25.

"I've got to find the bathroom, Chris," you fib. Then you dodge through the group of kids milling around. You want to put some distance between you and Chris.

A thick vine creeps up the wall in front of you. You notice a bright-green poster tacked to it. What's that about? you wonder. Why would there be a poster if nobody ever comes here?

You step up close to examine it. And gasp.

DANGER, the poster reads in bold red print. DEADLY PLANT VIRUS! Below the words is a picture of a plant covered with red spots.

"The virus affects most varieties of plants — *and animals*," you read aloud. "Highly contagious. *Proceed at your own risk*."

Whoa. Now what do I do? you wonder. If I show Mr. Denmead the poster, we might have to leave. Then I'll never get a chance to check out this awesome place.

But if I don't show him, someone might catch the plant virus. It sounds dangerous. . . .

"Okay, kids, gather around," Mr. Denmead calls.

Are you going to show him the poster or not?

To show the poster to Mr. Denmead, turn to PAGE 26.

To hide the poster, turn to PAGE 67.

"I'm going to drink this stuff," you declare. "That seems like the right thing to do. Besides, there's not enough to cover my whole body."

Your hands shake as you tip the vial to your bark-covered lips. You let the antidote slide down your throat. What if it doesn't work? you think. Or — *what if it poisons you?*

But the antidote tastes delicious! Like cherries. You swallow every drop.

You stare down at your body, waiting for something to happen. Your whole body trembles with anticipation.

You begin to feel strange. But are the odd tingles signs that the antidote is working?

Or has it poisoned you?

Gulp! Find out on PAGE 72.

"Crawling past them is too dangerous. They could catch us too easily," you whisper. You climb up the palm tree and grab ahold of a thick vine. "It feels really strong!" you whisper down to Kerry. "Let's swing!"

You watch the disgusting bugs. The moment they look in another direction you leap into the air. You aim for the door.

"Hiiiyyyyaaaaa!" you yell as you fly across the room.

One of the bugs turns its head and sees you. It opens its mouth and a long green funnel shoots out.

VROOM! It's like a super-powered vacuum.

The suction pulls you off the vine. You fly through the air and right into the giant insect's mouth.

Looks like the field trip is over for you.

SNAP, CRACKLE, CRRRUUNNNCH!

THE END

"What is it?" you ask, crossing to Kerry.

She holds up a small flask of green liquid. It's sealed with a cork.

You peer closer and read a tiny label. VIRUS ANTIDOTE.

"Wow! Bring it," you suggest. "It could come in handy if we run into that plant virus."

Kerry nods and slips the bottle into her pocket. "What else is in here?" she murmurs. She wanders along the high steel table.

"Something that smells really bad," you comment. "Come on, let's go."

You grab the door handle.

And it grabs you back!

Turn to PAGE 35.

"Help!" you scream. You shriek in pain. Your skin stings and burns where the goo hits you. You stumble backwards.

And trip over the thick moss sprouting from the floor.

The vine sways and wiggles crazily as it sprays the gooey red sap everywhere. It's like a water hose gone out of control. Everything the sap hits sizzles and fizzles to nothing.

The vine sprays your arms, your hair, your face. You're covered in the dripping, burning goo.

Is this that plant virus? you wonder dimly. Or is it just some weird, horrible kind of acid?

You'll never know. All you know, as you melt into a puddle on the floor, is that you feel like a real *sap*.

THE END

112

"Your idea is better than mine," you tell Kerry. "Let's break down the door. Where was that crowbar?"

"Over there." Kerry points across the ice pond in the middle of the room. "I'll get it!"

Kerry darts out onto the frozen surface.

That ice doesn't look too strong, you think.

But before you manage to get the words out to warn her . . .

CRACK! The ice splits.

Your best friend drops into the freezing water. It's horrifying!

"Help!" she screams.

You race onto the edge of the ice and lie down flat. You creep toward her slowly.

"Don't crack. Don't crack," you mutter.

"Help!" she cries again.

You try to control the knot of fear in your stomach. You chant to yourself over and over, please don't let me hear a crack, please don't let me hear a . . .

CRACK!

The ice is shattering!

Turn to PAGE 82. Fast!

Lush green plants and trees reach up to the ceiling, which is painted a deep blue. Colorful flowers line a tidy pathway. You wander into the rich green foliage. All around you, birds chirp and call.

"This place is so cool!" you cry. It's hard to imagine that right on the other side of that door is a dark, spooky hallway.

"Awesome," Kerry agrees.

You lean toward one of the brightly colored flowers for a closer look. You whip out the small notebook from your back pocket and start to take notes:

Tropical area — a flower as tall as me. Petals on the outside are dark green. Inside there is a ball.

You peer at the ball of color in the center of the flower. How should you describe it? It's red and orange and has the texture of feathers.

The ball looks like a little bird, you write.

You poke the ball with the tip of your pencil.

Suddenly — *BAM!* The ball flies in your face!

Go to PAGE 18.

"I don't want to risk poisoning myself," you declare. "I'm going to rub it on my skin."

You take the vial from Kerry and pour the precious liquid out into your leafy hands. You rub it on your arms and legs.

A fake sun shines down in the desert area. You didn't notice before how much heat it generates.

The oils in the antidote begin to warm up.

FIZZ! You hear something sizzling. *POP! FIZZ!*

Smoke rises from your arms and legs.

The antidote is burning you!

"Help!" you scream. "Get it off me!"

FIZZ! CRACKLE! But it's too late.

You melt down to the ground, in a smoking, steaming pile of leaves and branches.

You were supposed to drink the antidote.

Not fry in it!

THE END

Your eyes widen as you watch the transformation.

The plant oozes through your fingers. It reaches for the vines clinging to the door. It wraps tendrils around the thick plants.

"Go for it!" you urge. "Rip those vines off that door."

The end of the plant in your hand begins to move. It quickly wraps itself around your wrist.

Tight.

Uh-oh.

You can't believe how fast it all happens. In seconds, the plant morphs into long tentacles. They curl around you and Kerry.

Soon you're both trapped in a tangled mass of creepers. You can hear Max Creeper's booming laugh through the leaves.

Don't look so surprised. Why would the morphing plant side with you against Max Creeper and all those other plants?

Looks like you're stuck here forever. As entertainment directors for a bunch of plants.

But please don't complain. Everyone hates it when you vine.

THE END

116

"Well, now you've done it."

You whirl around. Max Creeper stands in the doorway. He glares at you.

"You've been exposed to the virus," Max Creeper informs you. "You will have to stay in quarantine."

Your heart sinks. Quarantine! You know what that means. It means you're going to be stuck here for weeks.

"But we can't stay here!" Kerry wails.

"I'm afraid you have no choice," Max retorts. "The virus is highly contagious! But don't worry, everyone will understand it's a matter of health."

Max slams the door.

You glance around the room. Great. No TV. No books. No toys. No nothing!

Just a bunch of recuperating plants.

This ending makes you sick!

THE END

You watch breathlessly. Is the bird about to speak?

"Ow! It bit me!" Kerry yells. She brushes the bird off her shoulder.

You snicker. "I guess that canary got *his* message across."

"Ha-ha," Kerry grumbles. "What gave you the idea the birds were trying to tell you something?"

"They were making eye contact," you explain. "And they all seemed to be screeching the same thing."

Kerry raises an eyebrow. "So what do you think they were saying?"

You shake your head. "I don't know," you admit.

You gaze around the exhibit. Dozens of birds perch on branches, on vines, on the ground. They all stare back at you. As if they were waiting for you to figure out their message.

"What were you guys saying?" you ask.

Mistake.

The birds all start shrieking again.

Turn to PAGE 68.

118

You dash toward the door. You leap over shrubs. You duck out of the reach of trees. Branches scrape your arms, but you wriggle free.

"Oh, no!" you gasp. You and Kerry stand in front of the door. But it's completely covered with vines and ivy.

"The plants!" Kerry wails. "They've trapped us. What are we going to do?"

You glance behind you. Max Creeper stands perfectly still, surrounded by his creepy plant friends. They're all *smiling* at you! And you're not about to smile back.

Think, you order yourself. Or you'll both wind up as caretakers to these green mutants for the rest of your lives.

Do you have anything that can help you battle your way out?

If you have the morphing plant, turn to PAGE 33.

If you have the bouncy grass, turn to PAGE 21.

If you have both — choose one!

If you don't have either, turn to PAGE 15.

"I'm going to press the unmarked button," you decide. "Because I don't know what W stands for."

You press the button, but nothing happens.

Then you notice a knob on the side of the box.

I have to try it! you think in a panic. We're going to freeze to death if I don't figure out how to turn this thing off! You turn the knob as hard as you can.

The entire unit starts to rumble.

"That doesn't look good!" Kerry shouts. Smoke pours out.

"I think we're in trouble," you murmur. The air conditioner is shaking and clanking and moaning.

"Get down from there!" Kerry screams. "Before it blows!"

You duck down and cover your head with your arms.

BOOM! The air conditioner explodes. Fragments of metal fly everywhere. They hit the walls, the ceiling, the door. . . .

The door! A huge piece of metal crashes through the glass panel in the center of the door.

"Quick!" you shout. "Go through the door!"

Escape from the Arctic exhibit on PAGE 127.

120

CRASH! A giant icicle slams to the ground. You leap out of the way. Shards of ice fly everywhere.

"I can't believe this!" Kerry shouts. She dashes out from under the air conditioner just in time.

CRASH! Another icicle falls. You race to the door.

BAM! CRASH! The icicles pelt the ground. The hot air has melted the ice that was clouding the glass. You see Chris outside.

"Chris!" you cry, wild with fear. "Let us out!"

When Chris sees the panic on your face he scrambles to unlock the door. Your heart is racing. You push the door open and dive into the hallway. Kerry is right on your tail.

"Nice going, Chris!" she yells.

"I thought it was funny," Chris mumbles. "I didn't know . . ."

"Yeah, well," you snap, "it wasn't funny. Not even close."

"Don't be mad," he whines. "Hey, can I come with you?"

"No way!" Kerry declares. "We don't want to hang out with you. We're lucky you didn't kill us."

"Yeah," you add. "And you would be in major trouble if we were dead right now. Come on, Kerry."

Storm over to the directory on PAGE 100.

"Trick them how? Let's tie them up! At least it's a plan," you cry. You grab the rope.

You take a flying leap and pin two of the baby bugs to the ground. Working together, you and Kerry manage to tie the three slimy things together.

But something terrible happens as you tighten the rope.

"Kerry! Look!" you cry. You can't believe what you see.

The rope is cutting *through* each larva. Cutting it into round, fleshy slices.

But that's not what makes shivers crawl over your skin.

What creeps you out is that the slices are changing shape. Turning into tiny little larvae!

"Quick! Stamp on them!" you shout.

You try to step on the larvae, but every time you do they divide again into more.

Let's do the math. There were three to start with. You cut each of them into eight pieces. Then you stamped on those.

Which makes . . .

This is one problem you'll never have to solve. Because by the time you finish doing the math you'll be baby food. Baby larva food, that is.

THE END

I'm going to boil this sucker, you decide.

The morphing plant curls around your body. It feels as if you're being bear-hugged by a giant boa constrictor.

"Aaaack," you choke. It's crushing you!

Using all the strength left in your body, you jump up and kick the water pipe. *CRUNCH!*

The pipe breaks. Hot water shoots out. It pounds down on top of you and the morphing plant.

"Yiiii!" You shriek. That water is hot! You squeeze your eyes shut. It's like taking a scorching hot shower.

"It's not working," Kerry screams. "The plant's getting bigger!"

Turn to PAGE 47.

"Kerry, stay back!" you warn. "In *Secret Agent Grandma* the roses looked just like that. And they turned out to be really dangerous."

"Whoa!" Kerry breathes. "Let's not take any chances."

You and Kerry hurry away from the rosebush. She points to a cluster of plants. "I'm going to check out that ivy over there. What are you going to write about for our report?"

Sometimes it's tough being best friends with the class brain and teacher's pet. You sigh, searching the room with your eyes for something exciting to write about.

Your gaze lands on the pond. "I'm going to take notes on those lily pads," you announce. "Brilliant, stupendous notes so that we win this dumb contest."

You pull your notebook out of your pocket and head for the pond. A strange sensation creeps through you.

Just like the roses, you have a feeling you know something about the pond.

Or do you?

Have you heard anything about a pond? If so, *turn to PAGE 70.*

If you haven't, head right for PAGE 29.

"P-p-please don't hurt us!" Kerry stammers.

"Oh! Sorry, kids, I didn't mean to scare you." The light clicks off. Max Creeper stands in front of you.

"I apologize," he says. "I thought you two were plant thieves. You can never be too careful."

"Well, we're just kids," you explain. What a weirdo!

"My father created amazing new plants," Mr. Creeper lectures you. "For the last ten years I've been fighting off spies and thieves who come to steal his creations. That's why the gardens are closed to the public."

"We *have* seen some wild plants," you agree politely.

"Yeah," Kerry agrees. "But everything turned out okay."

"Good, good. Better catch your bus," Mr. Creeper says.

As you hurry through the doors, Kerry drops her backpack. Some of the plant samples she took tumble out.

"Wait just a minute!" Mr. Creeper snaps. "What are those plants doing in your bag?"

The angry tone of his voice raises the tiny hairs on your arms. "What do you mean?" you ask.

Mr. Creeper's face turns red. Then purple.

"Plant thieves!" he howls.

Quick, turn to PAGE 27.

The stone floor scrapes your skin as you're dragged along by the furry vine.

"Help me!" you call to Kerry. "Hel — MMMPH!" The vine cuts you off by clamping a leaf over your mouth.

The vine drags you to a door marked BOTANICAL LIBRARY. Your eyes widen as you stare at a horrifying sight. A nest of thick vines reaches around the doorway, stretching toward you!

The vine drags you into the library. Other vines wrap around you.

You're helpless!

Turn to PAGE 88.

The hammer is about to crash down on your head.

Then — *SPLASH!* Kerry douses you both with ice water.

The morphing plant freezes. It is completely still.

"You did it!" you cry, breaking away from the plant's frigid grasp. "The ice worked! I can't believe it! Thank you!"

As you detach yourself from the morphing plant, huge leaves break off and land on the floor.

"I'm taking a specimen of this!" Kerry announces. She slips a piece of a leaf into a tiny jar and tucks it into her backpack.

You grab a lab coat hanging from the back of a chair. You use it to dry yourself off. "Let's get out of this lab," you say. "I don't want to find out what those other experiments might be."

Kerry nods. "There's the real door over there. That weird plant was just pretending to be a door so it could catch us."

You toss the lab coat onto the table. "At least I'll warm up in the desert exhibit."

Turn to PAGE 136.

You stumble over to the door, trying to dodge the pieces of metal from the air conditioner. You slip through. Kerry follows you out. Smoke billows into the hallway through the broken door. You notice that Chris has vanished.

"I can't believe we made it out of there!" Kerry says. "I thought we were going to freeze. Then when the air conditioner blew up . . ." her voice trails off.

"This is some field trip!" you murmur. "I wonder if everyone else is having weird stuff happen."

"Well, I'm telling on Chris," Kerry adds. "He almost killed us by locking us in there."

"Hopefully we'll have better luck at the next exhibit," you declare.

"Oh, no," Kerry moans. "We didn't take any notes for our report. Chris even spoiled our chances of winning the contest."

You know the contest is important to Kerry. You think for a minute. Then you check your shoes. "No problem," you declare. You hold your foot up to Kerry. "When I climbed on that rock, I picked up some moss. We can study this!"

Kerry laughs and scrapes the moss into a little sample jar. "Way to go, genius. Now let's find that directory."

Return to the directory on PAGE 100.

"Let's take the stairs," you announce. "And keep quiet! We might get into trouble if we're caught down here."

"You're right," Kerry declares. "This area is probably way off-limits."

Kerry dashes ahead of you toward the stairs. You notice something weird hanging down from the ceiling. Thick green streamers of some kind, you think.

"Hey, Kerry," you call. "Watch out for —"

Too late. Kerry darts into the dangling streamers.

They whisk her into the air! She hangs suspended by the thick fibers. They look kind of like tentacles.

You rush up to her. "Are you okay?" you demand.

"What *is* this thing?" Kerry gasps. You can tell she's trying to be brave.

"I'm not sure." You peer up at the ceiling.

Your mouth drops open.

"Tell me!" Kerry begs. "What do you see?"

Tell her on PAGE 53.

Kerry turns and races down the hall.

Even though you're terrified, you feel your heartbeat slowing down. Your whole body grows still. You can't move at all. You feel more leaves burst from your skin. Your trunk is growing. Your roots bury themselves deeper into the soil.

And as you finish the transformation into a small tree, you hear strange voices.

It's the other plants, you realize. They're talking!

You hear them chatting about the weather. The most boring subject in the world!

And guess what? It's all they ever do!

Being a tree bores you stiff! You'd give anything to be a kid again. You really WOOD!

THE END

You and Kerry take huge leaps over trees and shrubs. You find another door and bounce right through it.

"That way!" You bound along the passage. Kerry bounces beside you. Each step you take covers several feet. You are back in the main hall in no time.

But you don't wait for Mr. Denmead. You bounce right out of the botanical gardens.

You and Kerry get into big trouble for leaving the field trip. No one believes your story about crazy Max Creeper and his plant friends.

But you don't care. Because you and Kerry use the bouncy grass to make the most amazing sneakers in shoe history. You make millions of dollars.

Being best friends with the brainiest kid in school definitely comes in handy.

You and Kerry never get over your fear of plants. But that's okay. As millionaires you're surrounded by lots of green.

Dollar-bill green, that is!

THE END

The monster scuttles across the floor toward you. As it gets closer you see its armored belly and pointed pincers in detail. It looks vicious!

You huddle behind the chair. What are you going to do?

Suddenly you hear a familiar voice.

"Hello!" Mr. Denmead's voice booms. "Anybody home?"

The giant bug forgets about you and scurries back to the other two. You're relieved, but as you watch the disgusting creatures you feel the wave of fear creep over you again.

Those bugs are up to something. Something bad.

You strain your neck, trying to see what they're doing.

"Hello?" Mr. Denmead yells through the crack in the front door. "Mr. Creeper, are you there? There was a hole in the porch, but I put a plank over it. Can we come in?"

With horror you watch as the insects race to either side of the front door. They spread out the net between them.

They're going to trap your class!

Turn to PAGE 73.

"Hello, kids!" Max Creeper yells. "My father was a famous botanist. Your teacher, Wally Denmead, was one of his students. Of course," he adds with a chuckle, "young Wally was a troublemaker back then. I hope he'll be better behaved today."

Is he talking about the *same* Mr. Denmead? Hmmm. Maybe he's not as boring as you thought!

"My father created many new plants," Mr. Creeper continues. "He was a genius. But there were those who thought he was a crackpot." He shakes his head. Twigs fall out of his hair.

"I must warn you," Max Creeper goes on. "There's a plant virus going around. Avoid any plants with red spots."

Good! You don't have to warn Mr. Denmead after all.

Mr. Creeper turns to go. "Enjoy meeting my plant friends," he calls over his shoulder. "I've told them to expect you."

You watch Max Creeper shuffle away. What a weirdo.

"Okay, kids — it's plant time!" Mr. Denmead leads you all over to the directory. "There are four different regions inside the gardens. Report on plants from each area. Remember — the team with the best report will win a very special prize. Have fun! And please — behave yourselves!"

Read the directory and choose a starting place on PAGE 100.

You and Kerry dash over to the television. A strange old man with long white hair appears on the screen.

"If you have found this, you are in terrible danger," the man declares. "I am Max Creeper and I have done something unforgivable. I have created a new species of giant, mutant bugs. I was experimenting with pesticides and something went wrong. Horribly, horribly wrong."

You and Kerry exchange a terrified glance.

Max Creeper keeps talking. "All I can say is, I'm sorry. I have gone to a secret lab on an island where I will devote my days to finding some way to reverse the process."

The TV screen fades to black. Then it clicks, and the tape rewinds and starts playing again.

"Now what do we do?" you scream at the TV.

"We find our class," Kerry declares. "Fast."

Race to PAGE 102. And hurry!

134

You leap forward and yank Mr. Denmead's arm. You pull him down the porch steps as the planks under his feet give way.

He stumbles backwards onto the lawn. A huge, gaping hole appears right where he was standing a moment ago.

"Wow!" Mr. Denmead murmurs. He seems startled. And a little embarrassed. "The wood must be rotten. Thank you."

"No problem," you reply modestly.

Hey! Being on the teacher's good side for a change could come in handy!

"Nice work," Kerry congratulates you.

Mr. Denmead examines the giant hole in the floorboards. "I don't remember the gardens being so run-down," he mutters. "Perhaps this visit isn't such a good idea. Class, wait here while I go try the back door." He hurries around the side of the building.

"I hope he doesn't cancel the trip," you whisper to Kerry. "I'm dying to explore. When will we have another chance to get inside these weird gardens?"

"Yeah," Kerry answers. "And what about the contest? I'm all set to win. What are we going to do?"

Turn to PAGE 9 to find out.

"Cool!" you cry. You bend down and press on the thick grass. It feels almost like fur-covered rubber. "Kerry, check this out."

She hurries over to you. "What is it?" she asks. She sounds worried. You can't blame her. There are some very weird things happening on this field trip. But surely this grass is safe!

"It's really awesome," you assure her. "Watch!" You jump up and down on the springy grass. You bounce really high. The more you jump, the higher you go.

Kerry's eyes widen. She jumps up and down too. "This must be one of Creeper's special plant species. It's like being on a trampoline." She giggles. "It's fun!"

"We should take a sample," you declare. "Maybe I can attach the grass to my sneakers somehow. It would sure come in handy when I'm playing basketball. Or trying to reach the top shelf."

At last Kerry stops jumping. "We better head out," she says. "I'm not sure how much time we have here today."

"Okay," you agree. "But stick a hunk of this stuff in your backpack. I want it for later!"

Once Kerry puts the sample into her pack, turn to PAGE 100 to choose another area.

You and Kerry step back into the corridor. You walk down to the end of the hall and find a door marked DESERT EXHIBIT.

"This is it!" you declare. You push the door open.

A blast of hot air hits you in the face. But a sickening chill passes over your skin.

Because at your feet you discover a grinning cow skull.

"Gross," Kerry comments. "Check out that skull."

Then the skull jumps! Up into the air!

"Look out!" you scream.

Turn to PAGE 8.

About R.L. Stine

R.L. Stine is the most popular author in America. He is the creator of the *Goosebumps, Give Yourself Goosebumps, Fear Street,* and *Ghosts of Fear Street* series, among other popular books. He has written nearly 200 scary novels for kids. Bob lives in New York City with his wife, Jane, teenage son, Matt, and dog, Nadine.

Don't Lose Your Head.

GOOSEBUMPS®
SERIES 2000
R.L. STINE

Use it to scare your friends—to death!

#10: Headless Halloween

In Bookstores this September

 SCHOLASTIC

GBT398

PARACHUTE

GIVE YOURSELF
Goosebumps®

...WITH 20 DIFFERENT SCARY ENDINGS IN EACH BOOK!

R.L. STINE

$3.99 EACH

❏ BCD55323-2	#1	*Escape from the Carnival of Horrors*
❏ BCD56645-8	#2	*Tick Tock, You're Dead!*
❏ BCD56646-6	#3	*Trapped in Bat Wing Hall*
❏ BCD67318-1	#4	*The Deadly Experiments of Dr. Eeek*
❏ BCD67319-X	#5	*Night in Werewolf Woods*
❏ BCD67320-3	#6	*Beware of the Purple Peanut Butter*
❏ BCD67321-1	#7	*Under the Magician's Spell*
❏ BCD84765-1	#8	*The Curse of the Creeping Coffin*
❏ BCD84766-X	#9	*The Knight in Screaming Armor*
❏ BCD84767-8	#10	*Diary of a Mad Mummy*
❏ BCD84768-6	#11	*Deep in the Jungle of Doom*
❏ BCD84772-4	#12	*Welcome to the Wicked Wax Museum*
❏ BCD84773-2	#13	*Scream of the Evil Genie*
❏ BCD84774-0	#14	*The Creepy Creations of Professor Shock*
❏ BCD93477-5	#15	*Please Don't Feed the Vampire!*
❏ BCD84775-9	#16	*Secret Agent Grandma*
❏ BCD93483-X	#17	*Little Comic Shop of Horrors*
❏ BCD93485-6	#18	*Attack of the Beastly Babysitter*
❏ BCD93489-9	#19	*Escape from Camp Run-for-Your-Life*
❏ BCD93492-9	#20	*Toy Terror: Batteries Included*
❏ BCD93500-3	#21	*The Twisted Tale of Tiki Island*
❏ BCD21062-9	#22	*Return to the Carnival of Horrors*
❏ BCD39774-5	#23	*Zapped in Space*
❏ BCD39775-3	#24	*Lost in Stinkeye Swamp*
❏ BCD39776-1	#25	*Shop Til You Drop...Dead!*
❏ BCD39997-7	#26	*Alone in Snakebite Canyon*
❏ BCD39998-5	#27	*Checkout Time at the Dead-end Hotel*
❏ BCD40034-7	#28	*Night of a Thousand Claws*
❏ BCD40289-7	#29	*Invaders from the Big Screen*
❏ BCD41974-9	#30	*You're Plant Food*
❏ BCD39777-X	Special #1:	*Into the Jaws of Doom*
❏ BCD39999-3	Special #2:	*Return to Terror Tower*
❏ BCD41920-X	Special #3:	*Trapped in the Circus of Fear*

Scare me, thrill me, mail me GOOSEBUMPS now!

Available wherever you buy books, or use this order form.

Scholastic Inc., P.O. Box 7502, Jefferson City, MO 65102

Please send me the books I have checked above. I am enclosing $_____ (please add $2.00 to cover shipping and handling). Send check or money order—no cash or C.O.D.s please.

Name _____ Age _____

Address _____

City _____ State/Zip _____

Please allow four to six weeks for delivery. Offer good in the U.S. only. Sorry, mail orders are not available to residents of Canada. Prices subject to change.

SCHOLASTIC © 1998 Parachute Press, Inc. GOOSEBUMPS is a registered trademark of Parachute Press, Inc. All rights reserved. **PARACHUT**